for Vi[...]

glory of the English stage

and the Arabian Nights

with love & admiration

David Qutregard

فليب

The Comfort of Women

is the diary of a newly-appointed Lecturer in Arabic at Cambridge University whose mother and father die within a few days of each other. Shocked into an obsession with his amorous past, he attempts to locate the women he once knew, with mixed success. In a series of picaresque adventures across England and Scotland, David Quitregard (family motto 'Look Away') seeks, finds, wins, loses and contemplates the women of his Arabian dreams. His wanderings and his crisis, as a man of our time in a maelstrom of conflicting values, are at once touching and wildly funny.

In his career he sets out to teach the writings of poets, novelists and short-story writers from the pre-Islamic Imr al-Qais to the twentieth-century Naguib Mahfouz, and these figures haunt the narrative, as do the mystic Ansari, the rationalist Ma'arri, and above all the shadowy, obsessive Shahrazad, symbolised by a beauty in Quitregard's own class, from the Arabian cornucopia of tales we know as *1001 Nights*. DQ relives in his mind and in his life erotic adventures, hoaxes, dangers and infidelities in pursuit of the mistresses real or imaginary from his past, in Cambridge, an Essex village, Glasgow, Bath and Wells.

Capable of a number of deep but temporary emotional attachments, Quitregard is totally unable to maintain a permanent but shallow relationship. His quandary is that society values fidelity in marriage, which Q finds frustrating as he values infidelity and ecstasy. DQ is tall, handsome, 28, engaging, candid, and affectionate with 'other women' to the point of adoration. Disquietingly, in the 21st century, he might equally become a comfort to them.

This is his story.

قنوات في حدائق ممتدة بمحاذاة النهر لمسافة تبلغ نحو كيلومتر.
وقال المسؤول الاميركي «اذ لاستخدام الشخصيات المهمة ج وصفوة النظام وعائلاتهم مثل ﺳ وورلد (وهي متنزه في فلوريدا اعتقد انها مفتوحة امام الﺳ

ر الانتخابية الـ52 لانتخاب ﻧﻴﺎ.
يتنافس حوالي 132 مرشحا لجولة الثانية وبدأوا خميس الماضي حملتهم خابية على ان تنتهي مساء ماء.

والتضامن المحافظة الشعب اﻧ ان ينتظر الشورى أ الحكومة الشعب.

ﻋﻮﻥ لإطلاق سراح كنجي

خبارات الحرس الثوري في الاغتيالات السياسية في العام الماﺽ ولة اغتيال مستشار الرئيس خاتمي سعيد حجاريان، فانها قا باعتقال كنجي ونقله الى سجن ايغن».

وكشفت الرسالة «انه بعد تدخل بعض الجهات، تم نقل كنجي زنزانة القتلة والمدمنين والشاذين الى زنزانة رقم 209 التي تخضع لاشر وزارة الامن، ضمانا لسلامته، اذ ان وزير الامن يعارض اعتقال كن وتعطيل الصحف فاصدر تعليمات صريحة بضرورة الحفاظ على كن وتوفير ما يحتاجه من الصحف والكتب والأقلام غير ان سلطات سﺟ ايفين قامت بعد ساعات بوضع ﺔ (الماضي) تم نقل كنجي الى زنزانة عددا من اخطر المجرمين والقتلة وابدى زملاء واصدقاء كنجي الضوء على بيت اشباح وزارة الرمادي (علي فلاحيان). واكد مرض خطير في قلبه وكان مصا

ر كنجي بداء الى المنظمات «التحرك سريعا قبل قوات ابرز الكتاب والصحافيين ات التي تخضع لسيطرة النظام الشاهنشاهي، قال ﺮﻯ بصورة غير شرعية مة المطبوعات للرد على ﺧﺎﺹ الذين كان كنجي رائم البشعة التي طالت سة.
من ان تسمح لاكبر كنجي الاستخبارات السابق ﺍﻟﻠﻪ حسينيان وبعض قادة

قائد امن طهران السابق
نفي إصدار الأوامر بمهاجمة الطلاب

ن ـ كونا: نفى قائد الموجهة له في ما ﺑ ﺮﺍﻥ في يوليو (تموز الجنرال فرهاد نظري انني لم اصدر اوامﺮ ان بحوزة المدعي اﻟ ويمثل نظري و19 ﺿ ن الطلابي لجامعة طلبة وتدمير ممتلك

ن ﺪﺩﺍ امس الموجهة له في ما ﺑ ﺏ في حرم النظر في ﺑ ﻲ مؤكدا ﻩ قدمها الى لة الاقتحام في ﺳﺎﻳﺎ بين

مقتل عنصﺮ
ي هجوم ﻣ

ن ـ ا.ف.ب: ذكر نظمة «مجاهديﺮ ﺣﺪﻯ المدن القريبة من الحد ﻌﺮﺍﻕ مقرا يم عيلام ﺮﻭﻑ طوقهم ﻉ الثالث، بل اشار ﺮﻩ». واكد التلفﺰ مزيدا من الايضا

تركيا تؤجل البﺖ

برلين: «الشرق الأ

افادت مصادر في تاجيل اتخاذ قرار شﺮ في صفقة كان من المتوﺮ وتشير معلومﺎ ارجئت قرارها الى المﺰ حكومة المستشار ا لتسوية وجهات النظ بين الحزب الديمقراﻁ وكان من المتوﻗ الصفقة الضخمة ﺔ تفاهما ضمنيا بين ﺍﻥ المستشار شرودر ووﺯ لمناقشة الموضوع مﻊ وحزب الخضر الذي يعارض صفقة الدﺑ لحقوق الانسان والعﻧ ضد الاكراد في جنوﺏ السياسية والاعلاﻡ تاجيل القرار التركﻲ ثمن هذه الصفقة اﻟ السائد في تركيا.
وتفضل الحكومﺔ الولايات الالمانية خﺖ الحاكم.
اشارت المتحدﺙ الى موضوع تاجﻴ ان يعمدا اﻟ «من دون هو تركي بحث ﻻ

ﺼﻞ ثلاثة

David Quitregard

The Comfort of Women

el consuelo de mujeres

Philip Ward

The Oleander Press
16 Orchard Street
Cambridge CB1 1JT

A CIP catalogue record for this book is available from the
British Library.

ISBN 0-906672-54-6

Cover and calligraphy by Penny Price
Frontispiece collage by Bartholomew McMan

Printed and bound in India.

❦ 0 ❦

> ALFAGUARA
>
> A don Sancho Panza,
> gobernador de la ínsula
> Barataria
>
> en su propia mano
> o en la de su secretario
>
> 35 años
> LITERALMENTE
> APASIONANTES
> ALFAGUARA

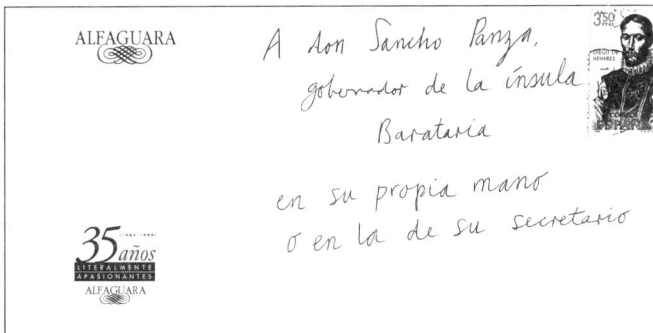

¿Quién es aquí mi secretario?

Yo, señor, porque se leer
y escribir, y soy vizcaíno.

Con esa añadidura bien podéis
ser secretario del mismo
Emperador. Abrir ese pliego,
y mirad lo que dice.

Who here is my secretary?

I, my Lord, because I
can read and write, and
I'm a Basque to boot.

With this addendum you could
be secretary to the Emperor
himself. Open the envelope,
and see what it says.

🎕 1 🎕

It should be one of the most important days of my life, and yet I can imagine that everyone will forget it even before it's over. Sophie will press her face to my cheek as I leave the house. She'll be harassed with Andy and Neil screaming and howling, guzzling and sicking. For everyone else on the road from Cherry Hinton it's just another Monday. But I'll open that door, my hands clammy and my voice just a little shaky, in a new grey suit. And

❦ 2 ❦

He entered the modern, low-ceilinged lecture-room, its rough breeze-blocks left modishly bare grey around all four walls to demonstrate 'truth to material.' The hum of conversation and giggles definitely increased. He cleared his throat and lounged, gauche as any student, from the door at the back of the raised podium with its chair, lectern and aluminium-framed double greenboard that could rise and fall like a pair of lifts in an old silent movie.

Apart from the Arabs, the young men and women alike wore shabby clothes, some in jeans carefully ripped at the knees, in fashionable shades of black, grey and shit. The men's stubble dated their last shave to forty-two hours before, and the women's skinny pallor had been clearly modelled on Ally McBeal, but without the cosmetics, apart from mascara: both sexes seemed to affect mascara or intolerable hangovers from vodka and cannabis. A joyless slouch must have been intended to convey world-weary sophistication. They had been brought up on pictures of homeless Palestinians and shocked by images of where the World Trade Center had so recently raised its devilish blunt horns. They had not grown up enough to become anything but radicals. They had been brought up – those Westerners among them – in a world they recognised as Peace, but now inhabited a world they knew to be War.

Should he ascend the podium like a god before acolytes? Should he roam at ground level like a mate among mates? Wave his arms ingratiatingly like a foreman around factory workers? His mind was made up by the crescendo of chattering. He rose to the heights.

'Could I have your attention a moment, please? Professor Oldeval, who was going to introduce me, had a fall last week and is confined to home, so I'll have to introduce myself. David Quitregard, Lecturer in Arabic, and I'll be taking the options on al-Mutanabbi and Modern Egyptian Literature in addition to some of the first- and second-year language and literature core courses. I'd like you each to stand up in turn, beginning with this corner at the front, and tell me your name and special options. Not so much for my benefit as for your own. You'll spend a good deal of time together in the first two years, and it's as well if we all get acquainted straight away.'

'Simon Abdullah Hartlack, al-Mutanabbi and the Qur'an...' 'Esteban de Garibay y Zamallos, Modern Libyan Literature, with special reference to Sancho Panza and the Green Book...'

Each fresher has come forearmed for a prolonged desert expedition, with a mobile phone and a supply of plastic water-bottles. This seems unaccountable, as they are within a few easily negotiated yards of a public phone, and within a gentle one-minute stroll to the nearest buttery.

'It would help levels of concentration all round if we could switch off mobile phones' (resigned sighs of genteel misery) 'and refrain from text messaging until the next coffee break. I remind you that, as you may have seen at the entrance to the building, all lectures begin at five minutes after the hour and end five minutes before the hour, thus enabling you to

4

answer calls of nature or cycle to the next lecture, whichever is the more pressing. Yes, Mr Klugman, isn't it?'

'Sir, Klugman Sir on a fellowship from Harvard Sir. I'd like exceptionally to be permitted in and out phone contact or text messaging Sir. It is the case that momentarily I expect a call from Pop about the Nobel Prize for Chemistry this year.'

'Who is in line for it, Mr Klugman, you or your father?'

'Apparently we both are being considered Sir as it happens at this time.'

'Very well, Mr Klugman. I'm sure that we can allow you the indulgence of staying in momentary contact.'

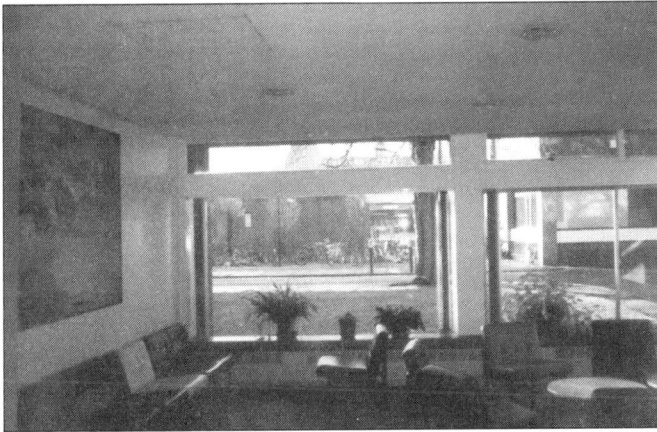

3

It's over.

'How did it go, dear?'

'Oh, fine. I wore a grey suit because Oscar Wilde says that real gentlemen don't wear brown, but my trouble is I'm a man in a brown suit dressed up in grey.' The redheaded girl in the second row knew it, too.

'Blanche Afanasian, Sufism and Modern Egyptian Literature.'

I don't bother to ask how a redhead comes to have an Armenian surname. How does Sophie come to have a name like Quitregard, Norman-French but so far back that our castle's been demolished and our moat filled in with rubble? Andy hasn't noticed anything special about today. Neil is asleep. Sophie is ironing. I, on this fourth day of October 2001, try to concentrate on a review for the *Journal of Arabic Literature*, but instead I think about Blanche Afanasian: her gold brooch and red lips.

'Come to bed, Sophie!'

'I can't, dear, it's only eight o' clock!'

My desires are divided equally between Blanche Afanasian, the approachable but unapproached, and Sophie the magnetic daughter of Major and Mrs Summerburn of Hunstanton, Norfolk. We never go back there without lashing rain or at least doomfilled clouds stretching as far as Scolt Head and Blakeney. The sea is death by drowning, helplessness, the revenge of water on land. I understand how the Arabs dread it, and ride like Imr al-Qais ever farther inland, to the safety of dry desert, oasis, cities in the sand built near wells and springs which give life without taking it back. Why are we not all terrified of water, after nearly suffocating in amniotic fluid? What is the hope in us that thinks we might one day get away from there – get out into sunlight with its minor treacheries? I make love to Sophie, violating the double bed of her childhood in the old draughty house on the heights of Hunstanton. The Major will never make any attempt to understand civilians, and Mrs Pauline Summerburn, breeder of alsatians, will never make any attempt to understand human beings. I am, in the house called Quarrybank, like an invisible heretic in the Prophet's Mosque at Mecca, left alone purely because I am never perceived. I once asked Sophie if her parents had ever made any reference to me, or to her choice of husband. 'They both think you're quite nice' was vague enough to convince me that discussions of my suitability had taken place entirely in Sophie's head.

I put away the critical edition of al-Ansari that I had been reading and dreamt of Blanche Afanasian's thighs, opening like rose petals, like her lips. The phone rang, and Sophie answered it.

'It's your Dad.' (She put her hand over it and whispered 'He sounds peculiar').

'Hello, Dad.'

'Davie, it's your mother. She's had a bad turn, and I think you ought to come over.'

'Now?'

'Yes, I think so. Right away.'

He rang off. Sophie looked anxious.

'Dad says mother's not well. I'm going over to Swavesey. I'll let you know what's going on when I've seen the doctor.'

As I drove the Honda Accord, rusting after four years of standing in our driveway, from Cherry Hinton on the ring road around Cambridge the few miles to Swavesey, my worries about my mother, and my half-blind father who depended on her for most needs, were irritatingly interrupted and smudged by the vision of Blanche Afanasian's copper hair and scarlet lips. She reminded me of a Moroccan dancer I had seen once in Tangier, greedily watched by every man on that dusty white street of the Kasbah. Then of an American redhead by a swimming pool in a Cairo hotel, her long legs bare up to infinitesimal blue panties. 'My mother is very ill', I said aloud, jerking from fourth to third gear at a roundabout near Madingley.

4

The semi-detached house in Swavesey High Street looked deserted, without lights. But Quitregard knew that it was only his mother who put on lights, and if she were in bed, or ill, nothing would relieve the darkness except for the headlights of passing cars. Early October chilled the hands.

The front door opened easily, as though bolts and locks were never used. For some reason he locked it behind him, and put on the hall light.

'Dad?' A voice called from the front bedroom.

His father had not managed to wipe all evidence of tears from his cheeks.

'What did the doctor say?'

His mother lay, deep at rest, in bed, diagonally shadowed by a street lamp.

'He's called an ambulance, Davie.'

'What for? What's wrong?'

'She's dead, Davie. A stroke.'

The son made as if to comfort the father, but the father turned away, ashamed of his weakness, his grief. They could not speak.

❧ 5 ❧

I thought I'd explain to Yukič, Professor Oldeval's deputy, that I needed time off for the funeral and all the other arrangements which Dad couldn't make because of his weak

sight. Sophie told me to phone, but as I'd had only one day in my new job I thought the least I could do was to tell him how things stood. He was cold in demeanour, conventional in his intimations of sympathy.

'I'll get Shambles to look after your lectures on the first-year core, and Runson the second-year. You haven't got any options starting till the second term, anyway. Sounds as though you might have to get help for your father. Might take some time.'

'How is Professor Oldeval?'

'Fractured ankle. Might be a few weeks yet. I'm going to have to keep clear of land-mines, aren't I?'

I went up to the Faculty Library to look for Blanche Afanasian, but the only member of my group there was Hartlack, from Worksop, a convert to Islam. He nodded when he recognised me, and after a quick nod in return I backed past the periodicals rack and out of the door.

6

'Shall we have Dad over until the funeral?' I asked Sophie, over lunch. 'Yukič said we ought to get him a home help or something but that'll take weeks to get organised.'

'I can't cope with anyone else if you're at home, with Andy and Neil to feed', she said, as though that ended the discussion. I felt she had no right to treat my father in that way, but aggression was unlikely to sway her towards my decision.

'I'll go over and get him after lunch.'

She said nothing. 'I've got to see the doctor, and make the funeral arrangements. It's the crematorium, she never liked the fuss they make at churches.' She said nothing.

'I'll help you with the dishes. Do you want Mrs Jallis to come and help?' She shook her head.

❦ 7 ❧

Seventeen was the number at the Crematorium. Quitregard remembered a few from sepia photographs; the younger generation from out-of-focus colour photographs. Others, he had never seen; of these, one accosted him as he was helping his father into the Accord. 'David, I'm Emily Pare from Swavesey, your mother will have told you about me.' 'Hello, Mrs Pare', smiled Quitregard, to avoid lying. '*Miss* Pare', with a hint of reprimand. 'The dahlias. You know, we used to grow them together. We were the best of friends. The very best of friends. Tell your father if there's anything he wants let me know. I'm at Boxworth End. I can come in and do anything he wants. He knows I was Jean's best friend. Her very best.'

❧ 8 ❧

As we drove off, I said 'I've never seen *her* before, Dad.' 'Who?'
'Emily Pare, says she's from Boxworth End.'

'Your mother used to go out quite a bit, looking after her
flowers. Asters, peonies and what not. Chrysanthemums,
hollyhocks. She used to bring me the fine ones to smell.
Sometimes I could *see* the roses from their smell.'

'You're coming home with us for a bit, Dad.'

'No, son, I'm not much company; your wife's got too
much to do, with two babies.'

'You can't manage till we've found you a home help.'

'I won't have anyone where Jean slept.'

'She won't sleep there, Dad.'

'She'll pry into our room, and Jean's kitchen.'

'It'll only be to get you a hot meal and look after the
laundry.'

'You see after Sophie and I'll see after meself.'

9

I tried to get some time to myself, but there was always Dad to look after, or Sophie to help, and I had to change Neil's nappies and mend a broken vase that Andy had smashed by hitting a wooden train. The rain seeped everywhere, and once I left the front door open so it flooded the doormat, which we put out to dry. But it stayed wet, and I imagined mildew spreading across it, like the blue flecks in blue cheese.

Dad started to go out for walks, but neighbours quickly realised that he was half-blind, and would be run over unless they took his arm, so brought him back into the house, closing our door firmly behind them. Sophie shouted at me for letting him go out, but I had to spend time at the Social Services in Cambridge, appealing for a home help. All the time I was talking to men called Jim or Ted I was thinking of Blanche Afanasian, my Armenian rose, my unattainable redhead, ten years my junior. But what are ten years? Arabs marry women thirty, forty years younger than themselves, and find no difficulty in pleasuring. I am conferring openly with Chloe or Jane about Meals on Wheels, but within me whir the wheels of lust for the coppery radiance of Miss Armenia.

And that other rose, Rose Calder, whom I knew as an undergraduate here, whatever can have happened to her? She worked at Garside's Antiques Shop in Trumpington Street. On my way home I parked among staff cars at the back of the Fitzwilliam Museum, telling the suspicious janitor that I was going for an interview with the Director about a vacancy in the Department of Prints and Drawings, and once round the corner into Trumpington Street dashed over the ditches into Garside's.

'Can I help you?' boomed a generous voice at the back of the shop, where discreet closed-circuit television turned the technicolour bric-à-brac into a still from an old black and white movie.

'Its about a girl I used to know who worked in here ten years ago. She was called Rose. Rose Calder.'

'Sorry, I've only been here three years. When Peterhouse doubled the rent old Garside moved away. What you might call early retirement. But then, nobody in antiques ever retires, you know.'

'Would Mr Garside know where Rose Calder is?'

'He might, or he might not. I think he moved to Pinner, in Middlesex.'

'Have you got his address?'

'No, but the Cambridgeshire Collection in Lion Yard might have it.'

It's strange to think I was pursuing this lost love, with sudden urgency, though for ten years I had only day-dreamed about the potential Mrs Rose Quitregard. We had met at The Four Feathers, E.M. Forster's pub though not strictly the nearest to King's, when I was ploughing through Tawfiq al-Hakim and Taha Husain. She was the daughter of Bryn Calder, the Celtic archaeologist, but had so hated the damp summers and autumns of windy Wales and rainy Ireland that she had devoted herself to the indoor life, studying furniture, silver,

Meissen, Dresden: anything that can be enjoyed by the glow of a roaring fire. She worked for Kenneth Garside, though she didn't need the money as she lived at home and spent her time at Garside's only because it was near the Fitzwilliam and she could meet likeminded people interested in old clocks and toby jugs. Calder and his friend McInally had retired to Donegal: no room for Rose, even if she had wanted to tolerate the long mists that dangled and trailed over the Atlantic coast of Ireland. No, Rose might have travelled, I guessed, but it would have been to the warmer south – to Spain or Italy, even southern France. She was a warm, cheerful brunette, and though she was a good deal shorter than I, she made up for lack of height in her curves. She was not like the other town girls, in awe of rooms in King's, because her father was a Corpus man, and she knew the Master of Corpus, and his wife, Lady Wrigley, who both looked in at Garside's from time to time.

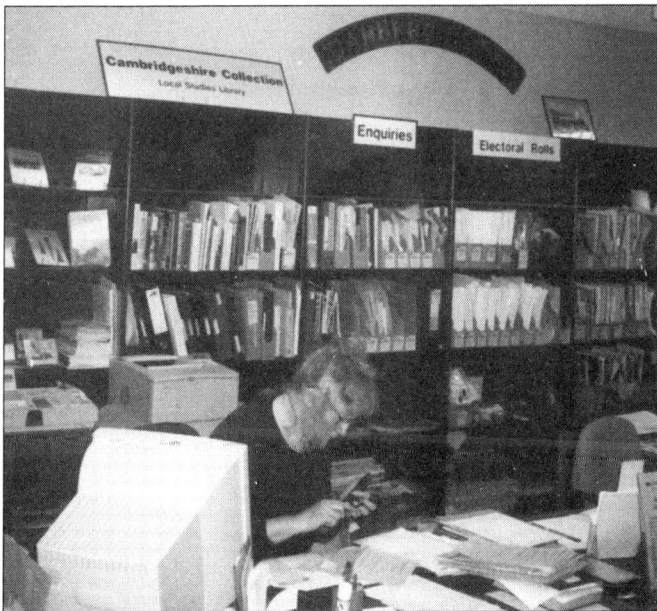

I didn't wait for the lifts in the Library, but pounded up the steps, past Lending, past Reference, across to the quieter area where the Cambridgeshire Collection was housed.

'I'm trying to trace a Miss Rose Calder, who was at Garside's in Trumpington Street ten years ago. Could you try the local directories, in case she's still single?'

No luck. She had either married, or left the district, or both. I fled, blushing, as though I had been caught flashing on Parker's Piece. What if the library staff knew who I was was and spread the gossip around? Quitregard is chasing an old flame... Bet his wife would like to know...

Back at the car, I drove slowly and carefully home to Cherry Hinton, rehearsing, 'It took a long time at the Social Services department, and I may have to go again ...'

Sophie was adamant that Dad would have to go back to Swavesey. 'He must realise that I can't cope with him stumbling over everything. He nearly trod on Andy. He nearly fell over Neil's playpen and killed them both. He says a woman called Pare will go in and could make his meals.'

'If you ask me, I think she's been wheedling her way into their lives in case something like this should happen.'

'Oh, don't be stupid!' my wife screamed at me, to our amazement. Then she quietened down, conscience-caught, as she realised that Dad must have heard that outburst. I know his hearing had improved to compensate for his defective sight. Andy came into the dining-room to find out what all the fuss was about, and clung to his mother as he always did. I kept complaining about the way she held my sons away from me, though if anyone was wilful, abusive, or violent, which was seldom, it was her fault.

I had given Dad my study as his own room until we could settle something definite, so I had nowhere to work in the evenings. I couldn't easily concentrate on al-Ansari's mystical verses:

The Prophet built an external Ka'aba
Of clay and water,
And an internal Ka'aba
Of heart and soul.
The outer Ka'aba was made by Abraham, the Pious;
The inner is sanctified by God's own glory.

What good are the words, or the meaning, if we cannot carry in our mind these firm convictions? And why these firm convictions, and no others? I remember answering my friend Josh at King's, when he asked how I could learn and teach Arabic without becoming a Muslim. 'You might as well say that someone who teaches vets has to become a cat. But I doubt if Abdullah al-Ansari was, after all, himself a Muslim.' What did he say? That the bewildering fascination of the world for a man is like a deer's thirst in the desert, which drives it to follow shadows of a mirage, phantoms of water, waving palms, and cool white arbours that vanish when approached. The world, writes Ansari, is dark. Life is a journey across a wasteland where the only path, of religious faith, is narrow and long. His only light is faith; his only food and drink are devotion. The way ahead is murky, and pitfalls abound, but there is no point in reaching for the candle of reason to light the way ahead. You travel in hope of reaching the illumination at the end.

But this illumination: is it just a blinding glare, like a sun's, empty of substance? Of what value can such a light be, least of all when we are dead or dying?

'Goodnight, Andy. Yes, Daddy will come and tuck you up.'

'Your father is going to bed, David. He wants you to go and see him.'

I trudge up the narrow stairs to the illumination on the landing. Yes, it is just light: nothing in it, or beyond.

'Come in, Davie. I want you to write out my will on this piece of paper they gave me at the Post Office. You get everything. You might want to get back to Swavesey in a house of your own, or you could sell it and pay off a good bit of the mortgage on this one. There's a bit of National Savings. I just want to say that it comes to your name and not Sophie or the children. I've nothing against them, but her family can look after her. These days they divorce as soon as they're out of church, so I'm taking no chances. Do you see, son?'

'I see, Dad. I'll do what you want, but it'll have to be properly witnessed. D'you want a cup of tea?'

'Not now, boy, I'm whacked.'

'Goodnight, Dad.'

'Just going out for a stroll.' To Sophie.

'But it's raining.'

I closed the door silently, and ran to the phone box. 'Directory Enquiries? Pinner, Middlesex, Garside, please. Mr Kenneth Garside, street unknown. He's there? Thank you.'

❦ 10 ❦

Next morning I called Garside's number, but he had no idea of Rose Calder's whereabouts, and seemed incensed that I should connect him with her name after all this time.

'Directory Enquiries. Professor Bryn Calder, oh: name of the place is Buncrana, in the peninsula of Inishowen, County Donegal, Republic of Ireland.'

Nothing. Ex-directory? No telephone? Try McInally? She had a brother, Martin. Martin Calder. He was a pharmacist at Addenbrooke's.

'Addenbrooke's. Do you have a Mr Calder, there? Martin Calder? No? Could you transfer me to the Pharmacy, please?'

'Pharmacy. Hello, this is a friend of Martin Calder's speaking. I believe he no longer works with you. Do you know where he is? Papworth? Thanks very much.'

'Papworth Hospital? Listen, do you have a Martin Calder working there? You do? Could I speak to him, please? Yes, I know it's his day off, but could you give me a contact number at home or a mobile, please, it's very urgent. Thank you.'

Please answer the phone. 'Oh, hello, Mrs Calder? Is Martin there? Oh. Where's Welney Bird Reserve? I see. Listen, if he comes home, could you tell him … No, it's alright, I'll see if I can get hold of him myself. No, thanks, no, it's nothing special.'

Heads I drive to Welney Marshes, tails I wait till he gets back tonight. But if I wait, he'll tell his wife someone's been asking for Rose, and she'll buzz buzz d'you know that poor Mrs Quitregard, well, I didn't ought to say this but buzz buzz. Heads I drive to Welney.

11

'Andy says you didn't say goodnight to him again last night.'

'I think Andy forgets.'

'Is your Dad going home soon?'

'I think so. But first I have to see Fred and Jim at the Social Services.'

'Who are they?'

'The men who work with Danny and Florrie. They're helping with Dad. Meals on Wheels, home help and so on.'

'Will you take the pram out?'

'Straight after I've been to see Fanny and Laurie.'

After all, what have I done wrong? I've not been unfaithful to Sophie. Or Mrs Summerburn would set the alsatians on me. Unless she was scared they might catch something from me. The drive to Welney could have been laid out for old ladies with frames who have trouble climbing hills; there's scarcely a declivity in any ten miles. Vermuyden might have drained the fens once upon a time, but boy you ought to see them now, as the Everly Brothers sang on a record I once owned. A drizzle and a mist so fine and all-pervasive that nothing is dry. Like a tropical monsoon in a refrigerator. Field after straight featureless field. No wonder the fen people are dull and flat, like cider left standing in a tankard. A funny place to be teaching Arabic. But you can understand why they chose it for a bird sanctuary: a bird would have to dig below ground to evade ornithologists hereabouts.

Blanche Afanasian, I wish I had blinds on this Accord that I could draw, to enfold you within, your naked body white beneath me moving in heavenly consonance with mine. Why do I seek Rose Calder when I could be kissing your lips? Because her breasts are slightly fuller? Are they? That was ten years ago. Has she had children, like Sophie? Stretch-marks are sexy, on the right woman, like notches on a hunter's bow. The Arabs are peculiar, liking virgins; the most experienced women are the least inhibited.

My mother dies a minute ago, and I cannot keep my mind off sex. Did anyone come to Welney before in the hope or fear of an assignation?

'One, please. Listen, do you know if there's a Mr Calder in the Reserve. Oh, I understand. It's just that I have to find a Mr Calder, of Papworth Hospital. It's rather urgent: my mother died a little while ago…'

This may sound odd, but I am afraid of birds. I didn't want to go into that Reserve. I went to Longleat and was afraid of the monkeys climbing over my Accord. And I am scared to death of swans. Not to mention my mother-in-law's alsatians, which honestly one day made me wet my trousers. I am terrified of swimming-pools, lakes, the sea, even village ponds.

'Paging Mr Martin Calder, Papworth Hospital.

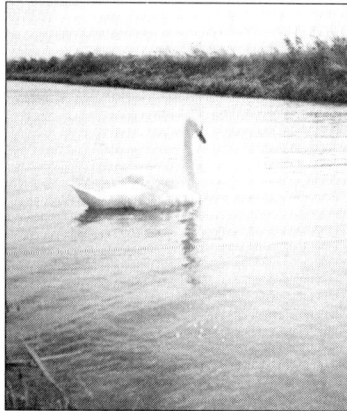

24

Would you please come to the Ranger's hut at the entrance where you have an urgent call.'

A tall fellow in a cream polo-necked sweater and brown corduroys came out not too fast, not too slow. 'Who's asking for Martin Calder?'

'I'm here for a lady called Blanche Afanasian, Mr Calder. She'd like to know where your sister Rose is, because she's got a diary and some letters that were lost and she'd like to return in person.'

'Rose is in Newport, I suppose.'

'Newport, South Wales, or Newport, Isle of Wight?'

'No,' he grinned at my stupidity. 'Newport. You know, just down the line from Audley End on the way to Liverpool Street. Newport, Essex.'

All those years she had been a twenty-minute drive away!

'What's her phone number?'

'Here, it's in my book. I'll write it down for you. And her address: Tithe Barn Antiques.'

I waited until he had returned within the bird sanctuary, and made for the nearest phone.

'Hello? Tithe Barn Antiques? Mr? Well, Mr Napcott, I wonder if you have a gateleg table … of any sort? No? Any tables at all? Chairs? Ah, that sounds just what I may be looking for, possibly. Are you open till late tonight? What time do you open tomorrow? I'll be there. Name? Just say I'm acting for a Middle Eastern principal, one Afanasian.'

Hercule Quitregard, you have located Rose. It's too late to go over to Newport tonight. I'll go home, have dinner, a brandy, and dream of Rose Afanasian, who is white and dark, redlipped, ample-breasted, with long legs that twine behind my back…

12

'Where have you *been* all day?'

'Anny and Dorrie sent me out to interview home helps for Dad.'

'Where have you *been?*'

'Centre of Cambridge and Welney.'

'Where?'

'Place in the fens. They have a bird reserve, and home help.'

'Your father got lost in the garden. Andy started screaming because he couldn't recognise him. It's time for Neil's feed. You'll have to heat the quiche or you can have it cold.'

'My father doesn't like quiche.'

'Well, you can make him what he does like then, can't you?'

'I'll be looking for home helps tomorrow, round Audley End way.'

'But that's in Essex.'

'Technically yes, but for home helps it's in Cambridgeshire. According to Sammy and Morrie.'

13

Wednesday opened the show with a quick tapdance of sunbeams on the windowsill, followed by a magician sawing the lawn in half (one bright, one ravenwinged), a comedian rattling 'I say I say I say' milk-bottles on a float, 'Ta, missus, thank you very much, thank you very very much,' and a slow striptease as Sophie removed her translucent black nightie and showed me, tall and unselfconscious, what I'd been missing for the last eight oblivious hours.

'Come back to bed, missus,' mimicking the milkman. She didn't reply, heading instead in unspoken reproach to the children's bedroom. Dad started to cough, raucously, then louder as if competing against the rest of a Proms audience. 'You alright, Dad?' Cough, cough.

Over the usual Marx Brothers breakfast, with Andy and Neil as the anarchic Harpo and Chico, and Sophie as the uncomprehending Margaret Dumont, I wisecracked over spilt milk, scattered Rice Krispies, thrown feeding-bottles, the scoldings, shriekings, and recriminations. When our teapot and glass breakables had been broken, they were gradually replaced by plastic unbreakables. The glass panel in the door had been shattered when Andy had backed through it in a fearsome rage

27

after I had turned the hands of a wooden clock to nine instead of ten. It had been replaced with an all-wooden door, which Andy had dented by hitting it repeatedly with a wooden mallet intended to inculcate dexterity by an ingenious manufacturer who, I hope, will rot forever in hell. Why don't we install wooden windows? Nuclear shelters were probably invented by people who couldn't stand the breakages at breakfast.

My father is only 57, but his sight is so bad that he frequently misses his mouth altogether. Little Neil is not old enough to find his mouth yet. Somehow the ages at which we are able to put food in our mouths are squeezing towards each other, so that soon maturity will consist of a decade from eighteen to twenty-eight, the years of co-ordination and sense between yipyip infantility and hawphawp imbecility. I am now twenty-eight – in the last Autumn before the tunnel.

I put on my new red tie, the one that Sophie had given me last birthday, to celebrate driving out to gather my Rosebud.

'I'll give your regards to Sally and Dottie,' and the Honda Accord took the road up to Stapleford, past Sawston, over the Duxford turning, and down the Audley End turn for Littlebury and yes, High Street, Newport. All the London-bound traffic now uses the motorway, so Newport is no longer the fume-blackened noise belt that I remembered from undergraduate years back, when I had passed through on my way to London.

'The Prince said, "O Qais, my brother, what are you saying? Love comes from the one God, and is not of our choosing." And Antar, beloved of Abla, added "The Prince is right, In the valley he found true love. No violence, no oppression, no cunning: simply gentleness and understanding".' Tithe Barn Antiques.

Park the car up on the pavement, lock it as if unconcerned. Push open the door; bell rings. Someone is coming. A woman. Rose.

'I'd like to look at some chairs, please.'

'I'm afraid these four are all we have as a set: reproduction of course.'

'Do you remember me, Rose?'

'You're David Quitregard.'

We shook hands like strangers, and my hand stayed on hers. Her figure was fuller than ever: a crisp white blouse over comfortable jeans, and open sandals.

'Are you married, Rose?' She nodded assent.

'Victor and I were married three years ago. I was working here...'

'The Napcott I spoke to on the phone?' She nodded again.

'Do you remember those evenings at your place?'

She smiled.

'I thought I'd like to see you again, and have a chat about old times.'

'Did you go to Lebanon? You told me you were going to some sort of spy school.'

'Just an in-joke. The old Middle East Centre for Arabic Studies. It's moved to Beaconsfield now, but I studied there in

Shemlan, on the mountains outside Beirut, after I left Cambridge.'

'And I heard you'd gone back to Cambridge when this Lectureship turned up?'

'Yes. Can I see you later?'

'What about? My husband's in the back.' But judging by the voice he must be sixty years old, Rose – what are you doing?

'I'm compiling a directory of beautiful antique dealers, and I thought of you first.' Her steady gaze transmitted: 'You left me when you went abroad at the age of twenty and apart from one bloody letter I've had no word from you since. Are you so sure I still want to see you again, after living without you for ten years? For richer, for poorer, for better or worse. In sickness and in health.'

'Tell your husband you've got to do some shopping and meet me outside the Post Office in twenty minutes.'

'No: not the Post Office. At the bottom of Gace's Acre, a couple of hundred yards along the road.'

Her husband called out: 'When you've finished with the customer, can you go up to Clavering to pick up Mrs Ovens' ormolu clock?'

The bell rang triumphantly twice as I closed the door. Ibn Hazm tells how as a boy he was madly enamoured of a slave-girl, but of course he was strictly barred from seeing her. One day, while the whole family was on an excursion to one of their estates near Cordova, heavy rains caught them unprepared and they had to share the few blankets between them. His uncle ordered the slave-girl to take Ibn Hazm a blanket and to cover herself with it as well. Ibn Hazm glories in that one day of bliss snatched from years of frustration. I kept the Accord's engine running at the foot of Gace's Acre.

In the rear mirror I saw her approaching: my Rose, of the affectionate handclasp. When we had been together at every private moment she would twine her slender but strong fingers into mine, meeting like wedlock, more than a hint of coupling. She wore two or three rings on each hand, too, which made the grip adventurous, with curious sharp, smooth or rough contacts that were never exactly repeated, even a few minutes later. She wore grey blouses, white blouses, maroon: never anything bright or ostentatious, as though her breath and presence were enough. Her dark brown hair I recall usually long, but on one occasion she had plaited it, like a schoolgirl, a style which took five years off her. This was a mistake, because she always looked younger than she was, and publicans looked at me hard and meaningfully when I tried to order her gin and lime.

What do I say to the face above the full white blouse? 'Drive to Wenden,' she said, before I could speak. We couldn't go back, to drive past the Tithe Barn and the High Street with all the villagers who knew Rose and her husband. We couldn't go to Clavering, in case the woman with the ormolu clock reported a stranger back to base. We could have driven up to Widdington and Debden, but presumably she was known up there too. Wendens Ambo was the nearest village away from prying eyes.

'Tell me all your news, Rose.' She stayed silent, but looked at me obliquely.

'Turn left, then up to the field: it looks impassable to cars.' But it wasn't. Has she been hijacking men off the London Road and seducing them in the seclusion of this spreading oak at the corner of a field in Wendens Ambo? What did it matter? I weighed her chin between a thumb and index finger and moved suddenly towards it. There was no resistance: could it really be as simple as this? We kissed more passionately, more expertly, and yet I felt in a way more calculatingly than our hesitant first kiss ten years before. Tongue to moving tongue, tongue to open lips, lips to moving tongue. I felt her hand at the back of my head, another stroking my leg. I caressed her breasts gently. She stiffened and tossed her head back, carrying my hand back to the steering wheel. An old man in an old brown anorak was walking his cocker spaniel. They both looked bleary-eyed and left us in peace, though I shielded my face, as if from the intrusive sun.

'Where can we go, Rose?'

'Nowhere.'

'I need you, now.'

'Where are *you* going?'

'I'm not going. I came to see you.'

Her gentle brown eyes conveyed the irony of our position. 'But not forever: you have not come here to reverse your life and mine, so that we should become ten years younger. You are offering me nothing, and asking me for everything in return.'

'I'm glad you came, David.'

'So am I.'

'When you left me… '

'I didn't leave you: you left me!'

Again the same tender smile, which overcame all obstacles – I think she could have knocked down a brick wall or cut a barbed-wire fence with its surprising power.

'When we lost touch… I went out with a Jewish mathematician from Manchester. We spent a holiday together in Tenerife, then he managed to get a research post at Princeton, and I heard nothing more. Strange: straight from an Arabist who talked to me about occupied Palestine when he meant Israel, to a Jew who could only talk about Israel (he never went there, because he said the taxes were too high)…'

'When he meant occupied Palestine,' I said, smiling.

'You've grown out of all that pompousness.'

'I've grown out of all the politics. It's true, I don't ever plan to visit Israel, but all the injuries of it has worn a bit threadbare, like a carpet you pace up and down thinking the same old whirligig of thoughts. I always admired the way you kept out of arguments. You said to me once: "I've never heard anyone say, when arguing with anybody else, that's right, I'd never thought of that, I've changed my mind because of what you've said, thanks for showing me I was wrong." I began to think, she's right, I've never heard anyone say that either, so it may be that as they cannot both be right, and so only one at most is right, possibly neither is right. I left the Labour Party the next day. I stopped paying subscriptions to the P.L.O. as a sympathizer. I stopped hating people.'

Her shining eyes wavered in their meaning, depending on the angle from which I looked at them, between 'Don't give me that line!' to 'Why didn't you ever tell me that I had some kind of influence on you?' After ten years away, one cannot be sure how to interpret any sign.

'Then I got engaged to a geomorphologist at the Scott Polar Research Institute: Geoff Tuck. He spent three months at the Antarctic, and frankly admitted that he found the Antarctic a great deal more interesting than he found me.'

'Even after three months away?'

'Especially after three months away!' We laughed, and the car seemed – suffused with gaiety. We kissed again, she unbuttoned her blouse, and unzipped my jeans. Her kisses were longer, and warmer. She had extended her repertoire with the mathematician, the geomorphologist, and with others that I should find out about. She hoped to make me jealous, to show what I had missed, and also to show what the others had missed: all of them. My tongue licked at an exposed nipple; my hand ventured to her groin, but some reluctance prevented me from unzipping her jeans, as though an offence might be committed which might seem unpardonable. She unzipped her own jeans. My fingers explored her vulva, and found it to be as I remembered it: *al-hasan* in the name-list of Shaikh

Nafzawi. The beautiful: white, plump, vaulted like a dome, undeformed, perhaps *abu bal'um*, the glutton, who knows? The bottomless, the restless, the vast one, the crusher, the yearning one, the importunate, the accommodating, the long one. My fingers touched relenting flesh, a moist tip. 'Believe me,' says Shaikh Nafzawi, 'the kisses, nibblings, sucking of the lips, close embrace, the touch of the mouth on the bosom and its nipples, and the tasting of fresh saliva: these things render affection lasting.' Rose reached her orgasm first, sighing heavily as she crossed her legs over my wrist; then she brought me swiftly to climax.

I thought of Rose as I thought of all women: slaves to a man's desire as in all Arab literature and society. I began to study Arabic because in that language and in that literature the sexual domination of woman is at its most explicit and extreme. In the early fifteenth century Shaikh Umar ibn Muhammad Nafzawi wrote a book called *Ar-Rawd al-'Atir bi Nezaha al-Khatir*, known in the west as *The Perfumed Garden*. With *The Thousand and One Nights*, this manual of erotic delight formed my sentimental education. Neither of my parents made any attempt to teach me the facts of life, and it was at Swavesey Village College that I sought the breasts and lips of young girls of my own age. I formed brittle, shortlived attachments with Glenda, Sharon, Celia, Debbie, Moira, Jacqui and Su. They gave away too little for a lad dreaming of whores, models, and film-stars. Celia was trembly, Debbie showed her knickers and ran away, Jacqui let her breasts press into my back and then acted as though nothing had happened. I had a crush on Miss Barradale, the P.E. teacher, and the French mistress, Mademoiselle Chevilly, who

did not show any sign of returning my affection. For three weeks I went to church to gaze at the back of Su Willis's neck and her beautiful blonde bobbed hair.

Then at a jumble sale I picked up for five pence a translation of the Shaikh's book on Arab love and sex. That night I realised what I had been missing. Instead of the coy hints and the dashes and dots which conceal writing about sex in the *New English Bible*, *Tom Sawyer*, and *Vanity Fair*, here was a man writing the truth about the pleasures of the flesh, which are as real and important as the pleasures of the spirit. Yes, read your Trollope and Austen, your Wordsworth and Wilde, but don't pretend that that is all there is. D.H. Lawrence says it, James Joyce says it, Henry Miller says it: the world may end in death, and gloom, but it begins in sex and sweet content.

Rose was the first girl who had shared that sex with me, that joy, and that peculiar after-sex melancholy which neither of us had understood, and talked about as though we were the first ever to suffer it!

The trouble had been, of course, that I knew what the Arabs taught, and what the Arabs actually did, but I had been brought up by a god-fearing English family to ignore what happened in my parents' bedroom until it was my turn to be one of the parents in another bedroom. What anguish, what indifference, what frustration is brought to a lad taught by the gutter press, the Hollywood movies, and the tv screen alike that there is a glut of gorgeous women waiting to be ravished, but as soon as he starts doing it there are cries of 'delinquent,' 'flasher,' 'rapist,' or just plain 'sex maniac'!

When I started to read Rabelais I found in him no uneasy disparity between scholar and peasant, but a wholly creditable wish to call a penis a cock, and a vagina a cunt. Rose blushed when I said the word at first, spread out on the Calders' lounge carpet one summer's night. Her mother had gone to bed, and her father was away in Brittany with one of his young male research assistants. As Rose closed her eyes next to me, silent, could she also be thinking of that night by the flickering firelight when I mounted her, and let my semen fill the condom before she had climaxed? She pretended to have enjoyed it, too, but I knew better after she had left me, and I took up with an Italian language-student whose boyfriend had just gone back to Ancona. She, Maria-Laura, taught me the heart-thumping rituals of oral sex, and later I sent her a postcard to her home in Pesaro with a coded menu including saltimbocca that only she could have construed.

I experimented with words. 'We met at the wrong time: it should have been now, before you married anyone else. Sorry: that sounds confused, but you know what I mean.'

'I'm very happy with Victor. I think we'll have a baby soon, but I'm not bothered about that, as long as he's happy.'

'Can I come and see you every so often?'

'I don't know.'

'I won't make any demands.'

'Where do you think it will end?'

I know where I want it to end. 'You're even more beautiful than when I went to Lebanon. You're glorious. We'd be good for each other.'

'Victor and I are good for each other. We make love three or four times a week. He's had a very unhappy life; divorced by a woman who ran off with his children, his home, the jewellery, all his money. The courts gave her everything.'

'Except the Tithe Barn.'

'No, he didn't have the Tithe Barn. His mother died, and he inherited enough money to buy the Tithe Barn and buy a few antiques. It's not easy. But we cope. So far. We've got each other.'

'Meaning that you had to have someone as well as me?'

'Didn't I?' Wide-eyed.

'Yes, of course, forget it. I should have come back a lot sooner...'

'But you aren't back, David. You'll never come back. And, if you did, I don't know what I'd do with you.'

I sneezed, again, again, again. She was obviously stifling amusement at the unromantic explosions.

'Could I see you again? Once?'

For answer she relaxed, closed her eyes, and turned her hands over, so that the palms rested on her lap, fingers curved up in a gesture near supplication. She responded passively, accepting my kisses and caresses almost as a wifely duty rather than as a mistress. She is 'letting me down lightly,' I thought, and wondered whether she was testing my sincerity. After all, I had left her once, thoughtlessly, as one may say goodbye to a woman met at a party – a one-night stand. It is rare to seek such a woman again: was she flattered? She must even at this moment be rummaging in her memory for signs of how she had been treated before: by him and by others. I thought of myself impersonally, almost, as a candidate for her time and affection, sitting ill-at-ease within but nonchalantly without, in a waiting-room, sizing up the other candidates. Pupils of her archaeologist-father, men she had met while at her Swiss finishing school, casual buyers and sellers of antiques.

In the far corner, slumped furiously over a Torah, a Jewish mathematician with a long beard, thick glasses, and a Woody Allen appeal born of helpless despair. Next to me sat a geomorphologist encased in ice, dripping water, grits of gravel, and fraggles of seaweed. Opposite me sat the stonewall, immovable figure of Victor Napcott, the marrying Rose-catcher, the incumbent, the short-odds favourite.

As my fingertips strayed inside her panties, gently and without insistence, I wondered if she had pictured herself at fifty, when Napcott would be eighty? Did she envisage his decline as clearly as she dreaded her own? She was too intelligent and sensitive to be trapped into admissions of Napcott's decadence: his twitching shoulder, stumbling gait, failing attention, sexual impotence.

'I wish I could see us two together, in twenty years,' I said. 'Wasting no more time.' That was a mistake. She gave me a dismissive peck on the cheek, and wriggled to dislodge my hand. The first orgasm had sated her, and she reversed her image to the prim wife.

'I'll have to go to Clavering. Don't ever call at the shop again. I'll put a card on the Post Office notice board if I can meet you at the station platform one night after the last London stopping train. The card will say TITHE BARN ANTIQUES 9.30 to 5; Sundays 2–5.'

'When can I see the first card?'

'I don't know. You'll have to come and find out.' Testing the warmth, the persistence.

'I'll be hoping for a card in a day or so.'

She pulled her white blouse straight down, tight into her jeans, shook her head as if to make sure her hair looked untouched, and got out of the Accord. I checked in the rear mirror: she didn't look back. Would there be a card in the Post Office? I could hardly come back every day to make sure. And what if her husband put in a card: no, the wording would never be exactly the same. I wrote down the exact wording to expect, and drove off home. But first I checked in at the Faculty of Oriental Studies, momentarily and by force of habit slipping the OUT sign beside my name to read IN. I collected my post: a subscription reminder from a scholarly journal, a letter postmarked Ajman but sent from Bahrain by a fellow student now teaching in Qatar, a letter from an old Shemlan friend now Second Secretary at the Embassy in Cairo, and a reminder about an invitation to speak at a Seminar in Glasgow which I had accepted months before but had prepared only in the

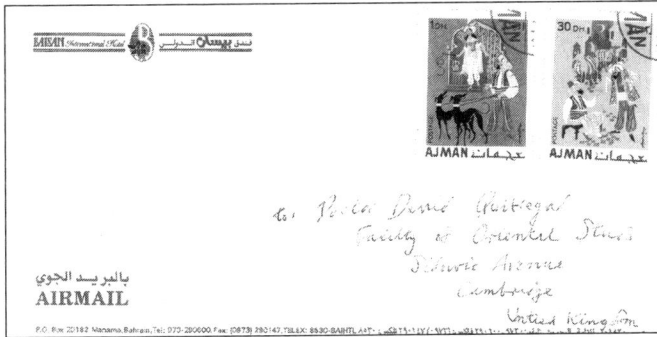

AIRMAIL

sense of rewriting an old paper, still unpublished, to deliver there in lieu of anything fresh.

Never worry about the Jewish mathematician or the Gentile geomorphologist. They don't compete: they are probably settled down with the calculus or a Falklands penguin. Nor worry about Napcott the ancient mariner, with the albatross of his own hoary age cursing his bent back, his thin white hairs, his scratchy mean voice.

Rose is still there for the plucking. I have this photographer's sense of seeing people and things in focus, as if they are to be snapped for posterity; but also a clinical autopsychologist's objective awareness of myself in action or poised. There is a woman, yes: but there is a woman who also perceives me. It is essential for me to understand how she inclines her head while lighting her cigarette from another; but it is also essential to infiltrate her mind to watch me. Am I dressed in clothes that appeal to her? Am I standing in the full light, with the left profile stating my place in her life, rapid as the movement of her mind may be?

14

As an undergraduate, the summit of my ambition had been to stand here, a staff member of the Faculty, with my own name on the IN/OUT board, inked in black on grey plastic: permanent, remembered. Is Dr Quitregard free, could you tell me?

The Faculty secretary was crouched over a computer with the caretaker. 'We'll have to call the engineer,' she said, 'I can't make it do anything but spell out a lot of noughts, then it rattles again, but it still keeps on spelling out noughts.'

'Is Dr Yukič available, Corinne?'

'I'll just see for you.'

Br, br. Br, br. 'No, he's not in his office, I'm afraid.'

'Thanks.'

'Message for you from your wife. She said to phone home.'

'Can I use your phone?'

'Sure.'

'Sophie?'

'Thank God you called. Where are you?'

'At the Faculty.'

'Your Dad's been run over in the High Street. They've taken him to Emergency at Addenbrooke's. Go round straight away.'

'Tell Dr Yukič my father's been run over by a bus and I've gone to Addenbrooke's to look after him, please.'

'Sure. Hope he's alright.'

'Thanks.'

My father, my father, why hast thou forsaken me? I know why you walked under a bus: it was to get away from me, from Sophie, from the boys, the problems, the loss of my mother, the emptiness of Swavesey, the frantic rush of change, the motorway from Cambridge which carved the fields up between Swavesey and Boxworth, the mindless developers who turned Bar Hill into little boxes, the big cars raced past your house by little people with loud horns. The greed and rottenness of people like me, who grab what they can before anyone else, then spit it out before it's chewed properly. The piles of rubbish almost new, and the straight cold stare of passers-by who don't care anything for you, or for my mother, or for the sunny, slow old Swavesey of the hymns and harvest festivals you sat through solidly fifty years ago. You didn't kill anything, even the slowest hedgehog on a path, because you never learned to drive, or shoot, or trap. You only felt a soft blind love for the chickens in the coop, and the rabbit in the hutch, saying nothing because any words were too clumsy, too lifeless to cover the vibrancy of what you felt. Somebody harder killed the rabbit when you were away from home. Somebody hollower had to wring each chicken's neck when the moment came. You were too young to remember the War, but old enough to grieve in retrospect for the innocent people of Hiroshima and the guilty bombers. You made no bargains with evil, but you were still bruised by its existence. You would not speak to God because He was responsible for whatever is wicked as well as whatever is good, and you could not visualise the Devil and his creatures, for above all you lacked

41

the ruthlessness that makes a man selfishly happy for a while at the races, in a pub, at a casino.

So you were constricted to the narrow strip of existence that only reasonable men of conscience claim as their rightful habitat. Without astrological fraud or theological casuistry or diabolical sophistry you made your own pact with the people around you, assuming each to be as reasonable and conscientious as yourself until proved wrong. How often you were proved wrong! My mother tried to shield you from the duplicity of your son, and even from her own needs. She sensed your inner softness: the fact that you could not, or would not, speak up for yourself in a crowd. You gave way, even to the demands of life itself. You gave way to the simple demand of the black lady who is Death. The black cloak on her. Beckoning darkness.

And I cannot meet you there: not yet. I have Blanche Afanasian reclining, copperhaired and willowy, crimson-lipped and sharp-taloned. The falconess to whom I am waiting prey. On the other side of Cambridge I have Rose Calder of my youth, a tiny mole on her left shoulder visible as I turn back the collar of her white blouse.

In the midst of death we are in love. But I don't know that Dad's accident was fatal. I don't know that he walked under a bus intentionally. I don't know what burden he carried behind his failing vision: what cowardice, what wounds from the Cold War of East and West, what renunciation from the jagged edges of awkward encounters with men and women that he cannot burden with his presence. He would rather not trouble Sophie with making his bed or preparing his meals; he would rather not afflict our children with the monstrosity of his disability; he would rather not preoccupy me with the problems of 'what to do next.' His contract for living was with my mother. When Jean died, his contract expired with her. He revolves the crystal ball of hopelessness within the deteriorating clarity of his head. Without his direct intervention, it would be turning yet.

But it was not like that at all. An eye-witness called Scoby told me that a Renault Fuego had hit the side of a Toyota Corolla as it had been overtaking a bus and the Toyota had been forced up the pavement on to a wall near which Dad had been feeling his way. Mr Scoby, who lived nearby, had hailed a passing Ford Escort, whose driver had brought Dad and his good neighbour to Addenbrooke's.

Dad was failing fast, in intensive care. He was alive, the surgeon told me in the waiting-room, but his heart and kidneys had been so extensively damaged that immediate blood transfusion was unlikely to prove sufficient. There was no suicide: it was just one of those accidents which seems part of a statistical pattern when they happen to someone you don't know, or catastrophic and incredible million-to-one chances when they happen to someone you do know.

I went to phone Sophie. 'Don't come over' I said, 'There's nothing you can do here. Galyon says it's just a matter of time, because there's as much internal damage as external. He hasn't recognised me yet. Tell the boys that Dad has gone home.'

When I made my slow, mesmerised, plodding way back to the intensive care unit, I found the situation apparently unchanged. A nurse inured to the distress of others, radiating a healing serenity, gazed untroubled into my worried face. 'Your father is receiving the best possible treatment, Mr Quitregard. We'll be in touch if you'll leave your telephone number, and visiting tomorrow starts at 2.30. Or you can contact us before then at this number if you want any information.'

'Thank you, nurse.' I trod heavily on my way to the staircase, needing strong contact with the ground as if? As if to feel the urgency of the earth's solidity as it sped headlong around the sun, with all of us, apparently unchanged, spinning with it in such synchronicity that we notice nothing. How little we ever notice! We need a biology class to teach us the intricacy of a worm or leaf; we need a car mechanic to indicate the efficient components of an internal combustion engine; we have to open an Arabic grammar to realise how the sounds of a language match its sense.

Very seldom, at distant intervals, we reach a state of awareness of a few of the things around us: the slant of a plum branch, a translucent earlobe, the sound of an early thrush, traces of jam on both sides of a teaspoon after it has been carelessly washed. But there is no continuity or real depth to these solo performances: we are irredeemably shallow, bored and boring. We drink tea too quickly, drive with our eyes dutifully fixed on the road ahead, not on the dangerous sideshows nature and man have contrived. But this day, with the death of my father encircling my head like a black helmet, I felt both preternaturally keen awareness of the kernel of things, and aggravated tedium in the senseless kaleidoscope, the boiling cauldron of unrelated facts and pointless connections. An old man, a little old woman and possibly their son, a fat baldy of fifty are getting into their white Austin Allegro. Next to them is a blue Fiat Uno being driven by a smart woman in a red belted suit with a comic feather in a chic hat, behind her a little fat woman in shapeless tweed talking fast and anxiously into a fashionable mobile phone, close to her head, as though confiding urgent secrets. No connection between them, or with me. Why do I detect every detail about them so sharply, when the crowds in the rest of the car park seem a single blur?

I looked at the steering wheel of the Accord accusingly as he got in. I shall kill nobody today by erring I threatened myself, remembering against my will that race from Beirut when service taxis parped and roared up the mountain highway towards Aley and Bhamdoun, that day when I found five cars smashed across the road, bent and broken bleeding bodies flung like puppets against the parapet, against the road darkstained and slippery with blood. That was the daily carnage of fatalistic drivers who never thought even ten seconds ahead...

I am to speak to Sophie of something that concerns us both intimately now, and ultimately not at all. There will be the conventional piety of those who knew him slightly, condolences unwanted as a stranger's Christmas card. Once I attended a Pentecostal church service in London, out of curiosity to see whether the worshippers were poor, working-class, and gullible. I wanted to confirm my prejudices, in other words. I did so, I was amused, then distressed, by the gabbling in tongues which the preacher 'interpreted' from the 'Hebrew,' the 'Syriac,' the 'Aramaic,' the 'Coptic,' and even the 'Ethiopic,' as though the bright-eyed preacher could distinguish one from another! Everybody felt rewarded by the hell of a racket; everybody but me. Nobody else wanted to consider the fraudulence of the performances, even if they suspected that it existed. But, why, they might argue, would people in a trance try to fool everyone else, when there was nothing to be gained by it but the glorification of God? What is wrong with worshipping God in any way you can? I have no faith in the existence of Allah, nor in the assumption that Muhammad is his Prophet. I have no faith in Buddhism and teachings about the need to abolish one's desires. Indeed, desires are like poetry: they are profound and incomprehensible. Nobody can explain the intolerable pressure on the brain of a few words on a page written by Paul Celan or Abdulwahhab al-Bayati. Neither can they describe the reasons why we desire to hear the Venusberg music of *Tannhäuser* or why one woman and not another increases our sexual urge to a point where we are willing to abandon all our habits and customs for the sexual fulfilment of a few minutes. I have watched transfixed as Barbara Stanwyck trapped Fred McMurray in *Double Indemnity*. I have cornered a brunette in the Piazza del Popolo in Rome, making idiotic conversation in order to remember the curve of her cheeks and the swish of her skirt. In Alexandria I started conversation with an American and his wife at a café because of the way she held her gloves in one elegant hand. I became pallid and tense with longing at an unseen woman's soft laugh in a railway carriage between Ely and Norwich, and thought crazily of asking Sophie if we could move closer to the laugh in hope of catching the laughing woman's eye.

Desire: what is it but the frantic passion of the butterfly for fulfilment? A real fulfilment, not the illusory promise of a Muslim paradise populated by houris, a Christian paradise populated by angels, or even that most impersonal of all destinies, a Buddhist paradise populated by essences. A butterfly is my teacher, as is a bee with its passion for honey now. A social structure entirely logical, yes, but based on honey.

I drew into my driveway, thinking as usual at three different levels: hunger for food and Sophie's body; preparation for the days ahead: hospital visiting and explanations after sympathy; and the galaxy of reasons and thoughts circling around my petty life and circumstances. Everybody lives in one or two of these three worlds for preference or by necessity. For the truly balanced life all three, however, should be kept in perennially adaptive equilibrium. I try; I try. Sophie attempts the second, infrequently, but lives as I suppose a young mother must mostly in the first. I live mostly in the third, with incursions into the second, and quick raids into the first for the immediate satisfaction of desire. Yet for some reason I keep Blanche Afanasian at arm's length. I evade her presence, as I might prolong ejaculation, and for the same epicurean ends.

Sophie is ironing, and doesn't stop when I unlock the front door and walk past her to the armchair. (She won't allow me to kiss her while she is ironing). I drum my fingertips

together, eyes closed and legs stretched out to mimic weariness. The mimicry is effective: fatigue rises like a fevered man's temperature in a thermometer.

'How is he?' Silence. 'Do you want anything to eat?'

'Whatever you can prepare.' She unplugged the iron and left for the kitchen. 'He's not likely to regain consciousness. Did you hear what happened?'

'Mrs Bullitt said that he was hit by two cars, and fell in the road, then he was run over by a bus.'

'If a blind man catches an elephant by a tail, he would swear it was a bellrope.'

'I can't hear. You'll have to come in here.' But Andy started crying for his 'Ganda,' and we never managed to combine our views of how Dad had fallen.

My urgent violation of Sophie's privacy seemed to reconcile us. After a brief period of arousal she parted her legs and guided me into her, raising her buttocks towards with both hands and clinging. I licked her erect nipples in a calculated pause until she pulled my head towards hers and we kissed openmouthed until the final jerk of satisfaction. We lived the secret fantasy of raped and rapist until the moment when I slapped her cheeks gently, one after the other, and she buried her nails in the flesh of my back, drawing desperate graffiti that would convince any court how bitterly she had struggled against her pitiless assailant. In the morning she would show me her bruised shoulders, legs, and back. We made the Trojan war of love, lasting years and years, the battles swaying first to one side, then to the other, until my Greek attack penetrated her Trojan defence, and she was dominated. Now she invented masochistic tricks: I had to smack her behind with a hairbrush, and pull her hair until she whimpered. I had to push her roughly on to the bed, and often tore her panties in my strenuous demands. She would whisper 'Beat me!' as I thrust deeper within, bruising her and squeezing her pinioned arms.

Tonight she coughed a good deal, and woke before it was time to attend to Neil with another fit of coughing that reddened her face. 'I'm sore. Leave me alone. Phone the hospital.'

'Can I have Intensive Care please, Dr Galyon's Ward? Staff Nurse, please. Nurse: this is Quitregard speaking about my father, admitted yesterday. Have you any news?'

A neutral, automatic voice asked me come in as soon as possible. There could be little but dread in response. Sophie seemed more stunned than I, as though yesterday had been a charade that would end in relieved laughter. But the parts of dying father and grieving son had not been shrugged off as one might discard makeup. 'No! No! L'autore ha cercato invece pingervi uno squarcio di vita. Ed al vero ispiravasi.' And the story, ran the English version I remember, and the story he tells you is true!

There are no short cuts to a man's pain at the deprivation of his father. He might go away to forget, he might drink consolation in the *De senectute* of Cicero, he might drink himself to oblivion tonight. But tomorrow the world is even so one progenitor the poorer. What he stood for may be vague or contradictory. He may have made enemies for reasons of his own. He may have been misunderstood by wife, friends, children. But as he was your father so you owe him not only your previously unique life, but those years when he worked and planned for your future, and shared no matter how marginally or obliquely the dreams that determine a child's destiny in its slow, irregular trajectory from swaddling-clothes to crematorium. A simple man, looking up to the immensity of space at night, needs no eloquence. My father, likewise, needed no funeral oration. I honoured him, and wept within though not a tear fell.

So much of my life had been spent in other men's fictions: the desert lauded in the Golden Ode of Labid, the labyrinthine rooms and streets of the *Thousand and One Nights* where Shahrazad could be heard singing her siren song but not seen, the Divine Comedy of blind Abu 'l-'Ala's peregrinations through Heaven and Hell three centuries before Dante. It was dazzling, even shocking to emerge into the light of a day which no writer had ever conceived, because no writer had ever known my father. I was alone, without a response. I thought, again, of Blanche Afanasian's shimmering copper hair; her open lips. I am never more outwardly solemn than when yearning for sexual fulfilment.

15

In a downcast daze I made arrangements for Dad's funeral myself, accepting with gruff thanks a well-meaning offer from Dad's brother in Scotland, my uncle Rennie. He said he'd come down, and I offered to put him up for the week. Accustomed to travel since youth, Rennie was a lifelong commercial traveller for a drug company. He covered the territory of Aberdeenshire and Angus, calling regularly on the same medical practices, shaking hands with worn G.P.s as they retired, and with shiny-faced new G.P.s as they filled seats left vacant by the elderly. The faces changed, the drugs changed, but Uncle Rennie made his sales and drove off to the next surgery. He had come south only twice before, and by air from Aberdeen because he couldn't bear to touch a driving wheel when not at work, cultivating his small garden with the zeal of a Tradescant.

I had once stayed with him and Auntie Cat – oh, I must have been six or seven – at their home in Cairnfield Place opposite the Hospital for Sick Children. The hospital seemed so immense to me that I imagined every one of all the children in Aberdeen must be desperately ill if they needed a vast edifice like that, with its jungle-like grounds, to which I added

Westburn Park on the side, and also I suppose Victoria Park on the other side of Westburn Road. I was taken to Nigg Bay, and shown Doonie's Yawns, Adam's Pots, North Broad Craig, Burnbanks Haven and Robin Hood Yawns. But there was no sign of Maid Marian or Friar Tuck.

Uncle Rennie had wrinkled and slowed since I had seen him last. He had given up golf, he said, 'for lack of puff' and Auntie Cat had been for undefined reasons 'unable to come.' He seemed distant with me, afraid possibly of Cambridge's reputation as a hotbed of intellectuals. He kissed Sophie, and fondled our boys with feigned enthusiasm, but he couldn't wait to get back. I offered him the standard tour of King's, and a walk along Trinity Street towards St John's, but he preferred to saunter round Cherry Hinton, the pond, then a pint at the Robin Hood and Little John. 'Robin Hood Yawns, Uncle,' I said brightly. 'Eh?' he returned, nervously glancing around at strangers. He touched his grey moustache gingerly, as if exploring fresh territory. His father, a lifelong sufferer from tinnitus, had once told Rennie that his incurable affliction was hereditary, and the salesman had listened ever since in dread of the first hint of ringing, blenching at doorbells, ice-cream vans, and the very sight of church belfries. So I couldn't, I recall from my parents' conversations a few years earlier, offer to show Rennie Cherry Hinton Church or ring to be let in when we returned home. Rennie said mournfully, 'I expect the winter's started in Aberdeen,' and that was his signal to pack his case, after the seemingly-interminable funeral (it lasted twenty-six minutes) and head back to Stansted for the shuttle.

❦ 16 ❧

Yukič had given me another fortnight to recover from my
second funeral and its emotional punishment. I told Sophie I
was going to drive around to be quiet, and I headed for
Newport Post Office, to look for Rose's assignation card. I
parked close by, unobtrusively asked for five first-class postage
stamps, and mailed three replies to those of Dad's friends who
had written to me with condolences. Then I glanced casually
at the board. Nothing about TITHE BARN ANTIQUES.
Nothing. She had stood me up.

I strolled down the High Street, watching stray leaves caper and rest at the autumn wind's caprice, in the direction of the Tithe Barn. 'Yes,' I said to myself suddenly, 'that's it.'

The bell rang, Will Rose be there again? The head of her husband stuck around the door as if disembodied.

'With you in a sec,' he called, in a cracked voice like Pantaloon's in the Italian *commedia dell' arte*. I relaxed: a clown like this – he probably wears plus fours in the garden – is no threat.

'Looking for something special?'

'Have you got a bussa? I'd like one for my aunt's birthday.'

'A watsat?'

'A bussa. You know, one of those earthenware pots used in Cornwall for salting down pilchards.'

'Yes course. No I can't say I get those. Wrong part o' the country, I spose.'

'Quite. I wonder if you and your wife would like to come and have dinner with us one evening next week? Or this week?'

'Dinner? Well, that's awfully nice, Mr – .'

'Quitregard. We've got one or two antiques that you might care to look at. Nothing of any great value, but I'd value your opinion.'

'Certainly. What day, time?'

'Say next Monday, 6.50 for 7.30.'

'Right. What address, and phone number?'

I gave him my address, but kept the phone number secret so that Rose couldn't ring up Sophie and cancel it. I was listening for sounds of Rose, but heard only the dull thuds of clock after clock pounding away the minutes without her.'

'Cheerio then. Mr Napcott, isn't it?'

'I'll keep Monday evening free,' and he waved like a clumsy over-arm bowler at the moment of releasing the ball. No threat. I had avoided repeating 'Do remember to bring your wife along,' so he could have no suspicion. She could be introduced into the household, and out of jealousy of Sophie she would fall into my eager arms again. The girl I had lost ten years before would lie beneath me as she had done on the rug illuminated by flame from her family's fire.

What dress would she wear? How would her makeup compare with Sophie's? Would Sophie sense that a rival tigress was entering the territory of my pride? How could it be otherwise, if I were to glance coolly from one to the other? It is not that I am a philanderer. I have no paranoid Don Juan tendency to master any woman I meet, 'se sia ricca, brutta, se sia bella.' Nor have I stayed single-mindedly single, unlike Casanova, who said that he loved women even to madness, but he loved liberty more, and whenever he had been in danger of losing liberty, he had been spared only by chance. I would save marriage from its detractors, but I would save infidelity from those who would wipe out that true piquancy of married life, the secret affair, the hidden love-letter, the stolen moments in the night when the other sleeps.

How could I ever forget that delicious adventure on our honeymoon, when Sophie had gone out shopping in Kensington High Street, leaving me in the hotel on my own? Three hours to spare, and in the next room a buxom Dutch woman of fifty had been left while her husband had gone to the City on business. It was my first uncertain step in the connoisseurship of infidelity, and my mouth was dry. I was twenty-four and must have seemed callow to the spirited lady next door.

I knocked on her door, and she smiled at me. I said 'May I come in? I'd like some advice,' blushing and hesitating. 'What is it?' she asked, furrowing her brow. Straightening my tie, as she pulled her shoulders back slightly to correct a slight stoop, I was aware of the first hint of courtship in both movements. I was in another woman's bedroom by her invitation, and took her hand. She withdrew it instantly: my first mistake.

'I am on my honeymoon,' I said, 'and I'm afraid I'm not very good at making love. I thought perhaps…'

'You thought that I am a woman of a certain experience?'

'I think you're very beautiful,' I declared, semi-seriously, and indeed her wavy hair and full figure made the difference in our ages seem insignificant. 'Could you show me how I could make my wife more happy? I can get satisfaction, but I need to feel that she is also satisfied.'

She gently brought my head down to hers with the palm of her right hand, and with her left she guided my own between her legs. As she kissed me open-mouthed she parted her legs. I pretended to be clumsier than natural in order to increase her zeal as a teacher with a backward pupil. She unzipped her skirt, and it fell to the floor. I tried to undo the buttons on her blouse but she shook her head. 'I am going to have a mastectomy,' she said softly, with that clear English accent that only the Dutch and Danes can master: it sounds better than our own. 'But I shall show you how to give pleasure to your wife.'

After orgasm she bent down to kiss my chest, my stomach, my legs. Her tongue licked passionately until it found a mounting tension, a hardness which she enhanced by the pressure of her fingers and the urgency of her mouth.

At the end she held my hand tightly, as if we were bound indissolubly, without knowing each other's name, without mentioning any hope to meet again. The sadness of parting from those we have loved once is so unbearable that I could wish nobody such lorn bitterness. Who was she? Nobody can ever know, because even if I were to tramp the streets of every Dutch town, one after the other, we should never meet again. It is perhaps not her I have lost, but the sweetest memory of a generous woman who saw in a transient affair the means of

55

giving a simple, sudden joy to a man who had not deserved it. I closed the door behind me, and instead of going out into Kensington High Street I undressed again and went back to sleep.

Even the vision of Blanche Afanasian washing her body in the bath could not help me to concentrate. Everything was geared to the dinner party on Monday evening, which Sophie had agreed to prepare only after endless complaints and questions. Why did we need to sell our antiques? We only had a few, and they had been carefully chosen, some of them together. A few were family heirlooms from her side which I was enjoined not to show at all. And why Napcott from Newport, of all places, instead of the local dealers in Cambridge? And why couldn't he come round during business hours: blay, blay, blay. Some of the complaints I answered quietly and reasonably. Those I didn't answer I shrugged off with the throwaway line 'What does it matter? If we don't like the offers he makes, we can turn them down. Why is it such a problem?'

On Monday evening everything was prepared, sherry and white wine ready, and ten minutes late their car arrived. I could have spat nine snakes – he had not brought Rose. I was landed with an evening suddenly lacking female rivalry. We could all relax.

Victor Napcott was a man of opinions. Few, vehemently held, and wrong. I liked him instantly, and forgave his insufferable egotism, his determination to cap everyone else's stories, and his banal views on whatever he chose to consider important. The rest of the world (and there was a lot he did not cover in his thoughts or words or deeds) he considered, to use his favourite word 'trivial.' After listening to Sophie on the theme of the high cost of children's clothes, he actually asked 'Is it important, or can I forget it all?' No boobies so tactless and boorish can be all bad, because for one thing they are neither calculating nor cunning. Their egotism is straightforward and transparent. They might punch you on the jaw, but they would never stick a knife in your back. Napcott had been a major in the Army until invalided out with chronic rheumatism. He had built up an antiques business in Braintree, but then his wife had divorced him, and he had lost not only his family and most of his possessions, as Rose had told me earlier, but clearly also his self-respect. A life had been ripped from under him like a waiter pulling the tablecloth trick. He said nothing of this, but it resonated in his loud opinions. 'Ban the Euro from every shop in Britain.' 'Send the wogs home, there's no room for them here.' Then 'Dig up the motorways and hand the land back to the railway companies.' His face was flushed: he clearly could not take too much alcohol. Long hairs straggled out of his bulbous nose like wispy lemmings rushing to the sea frozen in the act. His elbows shook as eloquently as a conductor's baton. He shook his head to mean 'yes,' 'no,' and 'maybe,' confusing everybody as if he were a foreigner unaccustomed to our gestures. He ate his food with the concentrated passion of a drug addict snorting heroin: he clearly ate at odd times, and at one point told us so. He quivered with fear about air attacks by Usama bin Ladin's terrorists.

'Eating's trivial. As long as you get enough, any time is mealtime. What matters is that your time's your own. People only think about money, but we all get more or less enough money. We just don't get enough time. I divide people into two types: slaves and masters. Slaves are people like bank clerks, the royal family, farmers, those breakfast TV people, businessmen who work an eighty hour week. Masters are people like sculptors, gypsies, dentists, who do work they like when they want to do it, and never have to be tied down to a routine. Do you do what you want to do? You're a master. Do you do what's expected of you by other people? You're a slave.'

Sophie said: 'I don't see how you can say that a mother and housewife like me can be a master or a slave. We have to do our routine for part of the time, but there's several hours in the day when we can do what we want.'

I added in her defence: 'A dentist may be able to do only a few hours work in a week, but when he's working, I don't see that he necessarily enjoys what he's doing.'

Napcott stated: 'The argument's trivial. A housewife is a master, because she can pick her own timetable, choose her own friends, read in the morning if she wants to do the laundry in the evening. You can always tell the masters: they read books, buy books, borrow books, write books. Slaves are too preoccupied with doing what they're told to take time off for reading. Look at the Leader of the Opposition: can he spend a weekend with Tolstoy or Dostoevsky? No. But a scholar can. Politicians are all slaves, and scholars are all masters. A G.P. still practising is a slave; a retired G.P. is a master, stands to reason. Some people like being a slave because it gives them a place in society, a recognised function, a status like being boss of a nationalised industry or his trade union opponent.'

I asked him how to turn slaves into masters.

'For God's sake don't do it. If they ever found out they were on a treadmill, like a hamster in a cage, they'd scream in unison and shatter the earth's crust with their howling. They're too busy to think: that's the sign of a slave. When he begins to think, which is usually when he begins to read, he plans how to switch from slavery to mastery. That's why stockbrokers stop commuting to the City of London from Dorking, and start a career hiring out boats on the Norfolk Broads.'

His elbows quaked as though he were a fledgling plucking up courage to fly for the first time. His nostrils quivered, and the long hairs vibrated from them.

'In the antiques business, you can do as much work or as little as you like every day. You attend sales if you want to, or show at fairs, or call on potential sellers. You visit country houses and National Trust properties for pleasure, and learn a bit about your job. You can read textbooks on clocks and prints, or you can specialise in Chippendale real or reproduction. You can live almost anywhere you want, the prettier the better, because tourists come without being coaxed. You can open three days a week, or seven. Nobody's more of a master than an antiques dealer. You can see the jealousy in the eyes of slaves who come into your shop.'

'Does a timetable to teach Arabic literature make me a slave?'

'Shouldn't think so, old man, what with all those weeks of summer vacation. Cushy life, eh?'

'I didn't set out to become a Lecturer in Arabic.'

'No?'

'No. After Swavesey Village College I did Classics at the Leys in the Sixth Form, then they told me there were no prospects for Classicists, so I did Arabic at Cambridge, with the interpreter's course in Lebanon, and when a vacancy came up here they told me I'd be a fool not to take it. So I took it. Seems I'm a pawn in the events on the chessboard. A slave.'

Sophie said: 'I don't know. I think a lot of people would envy you.'

'Mr Napcott here thinks that a lot of people envy the royal family, but they are so cluttered with ritual and routine that they probably have as little leisure as pandas at the zoo. Trapped, watched, photographed, and endlessly discussed, but never once able to make an independent decision without considering the consequences.'

'It's a great advantage,' burped Napcott, putting his knuckles against his mouth without managing to conceal the wind, 'to have a face that nobody recognises. I'm always grateful that my mother wasn't the Duchess of Blancmange.' I let the bore talk on. If you argue, they only bore more, Rose had quietly and presciently whispered once before, so keep quiet and they'll stop. That's the Cambridge method. The Oxford method is to argue into nights of flickering candles: then you get the novels of Iris Murdoch.

No threat. I watched the endearing fellow as he hiccuped and belched his way through coffee and After Eights. I had a crazy impulse to leave them both and go after Rose, but soberly rejected it as melodramatic.

'Are you going to be on the road, at sales and things, much, Mr Napcott. Or is the season over?'

'Call me Victor. No, I just have a trip to Buntingford and Furneux Pelham on Thursday. I'm mainly doing a bit of restoration: I'm quite a specialist in early clocks, and that keeps me busy enough.'

I yawned and clattered the crockery to hint that his visit had lasted amply long enough. I thought of his goggle eyes if confronted with the splendid bosom of Blanche Afanasian and her fiery arcane eyes. She is enough to lift your soul to the heights where torment becomes ecstasy, *ya akh* Napcott. As he got into his estate car I toyed with the notion of tampering with his brakes, so that Rose would become a Merry Widow, but resisted the idea. My reactions are too slow for an acquittable murderer; you can't pluck up sufficient evil to do away with a man whose elbows vibrate like bellows. Saliva glistened on his stubbly chin. He was aimlessly belligerent: the patron saint of mediocrity. Let all telephonists and insurance salesmen cross themselves at the sight of your grinning, fatuous portrait, Saint Victor Napcott. You'll never do any harm because you'll never risk doing anyone any good. Why don't you invite us back so we can delight in the home cooking of your scented, full bosomed wife, the incomparable Rose?

Sophie had cleared away the dishes while I was dismissing the farcical Victor from our driveway, and hissing away two local cats whose nightly rendezvous had brought them below his vehicle. But she didn't start to wash the dishes until I returned, humming the decibel-level that would waken the boys. I stroked her breasts but she was thinking about her shopping list; I kissed the nape of her neck, but she felt irritated that I was not drying the dishes; I cupped her buttocks in my palms, but she walked abruptly away, leaving my hands like a wicket-keeper's when expecting delivery.

🐦 17 🐦

'Aren't you going to Grange Road?' she said, from the doorway.
I remembered that I had a tennis match against Batty McMan,
and picked up my sports bag.

As I drove towards Grange Road tennis court, for one of
those dreamlike evening ladder games mainly involving Clare,
King's and Trinity men, I wondered what enormity Batty had
thought up that day. The only living hoaxer to be
immortalised in Frank Reeve's *Varsity Rags and Hoaxes*, Batty
had recently been uncovered as the culprit behind a false
prospectus sent out to American campuses to offer summer
courses at Fisher College, a Cambridge seat of learning
invented by Glyn Daniel in *The Cambridge Murders*. He is
even now worshipped by a tribe of Northern Territory
aborigines who picked up table-tennis balls dropped by Batty
from a hot air balloon he had rented from a television crew in
Brisbane. Batty is one of those souls, like mountaineers, who
express themselves only by what they do, not by what they are.
Disdained by the Tennis Committee who saw their sport as
solemnity became sacrosanct, Batty oddly enough took tennis
more seriously than anything else in life, especially than his
father's hi-tech business on Cambridge Science Park which he

had joined after leaving Trinity Hall without anything better than a 2.2. He was a very good player, giving me three bisques, and had fully deserved his quarter blues against Oxford in two successive years, when Ossie de Vere Tollemache captained the team.

Batty had married a five-foot waif called Lizzie whom he idolised as if she were a Dresden shepherdess, and she had given birth to twins, Leo and Ruth, over whom he waxed peculiarly enthusiastic.

I had been invited for their christening to Westley Waterless, where his uncle was Vicar. Batty knew most people socially, but was curiously ignorant about what they did, for he professed never to open a newspaper or listen to radio or TV news. He was convinced David Beckham was a cricketer, and in Jersey had struck up friendship with a feller he described as Alan Wickett – seemed to be a boasting man.

Batty's hoaxing seemed to compensate for his dull home life and tedious working environment; on his annual holidays he made up for life's monotony by such exploits as visiting Antarctica with papier mâché models of the Kremlin and the Pentagon, which he would photograph against pack ice, sending the results with prepared press releases to UPI and Reuters under such headlines as PENTAGON ENGULFED IN ICE or KREMLIN: THE COLDEST WAR!

His most dangerous adventure had been to 'defect' to North Korea with microfilms he declared to be of immense value to the Dear Leader. When opened by the authorities and found to be blank he cursed the security equipment at Pyongyang airport which, he claimed, had ruined ten years' work in exposing double agents in MI5 and MI6. The Koreans had held him for ten days before prudently deciding that he would be of more danger to Britain at home than abroad, and deporting him to a frosty but luckily unpublicised reception committee at Heathrow, where he was 'debriefed' and warned on pain of Official Secrets prosecution not to do it again.

One afternoon, at the Albert Hall, by an ingenious though still unpublished ploy, he and a group of cronies had for five hours decoyed away Simon Rattle from rehearsals with a combined schools orchestra, and taken his place, though nobody was any the wiser after the effective impersonation. Even now nobody believes that the photos taken that afternoon were not of the boyish maestro, but of the wholly unmistakable Batty McMan. The incident was struck from Rattle's biography.

For the benefit of tourists to King's College Chapel, Batty had devised a cleverly-scripted play in which an associate in the guide of a college gardener drew his pistol on Batty, in the robes of a Senior Fellow, and after melodramatic flourishes presumably based on *East Lynne* or *Maria Marten*, accused the Senior Fellow of raping his wife, killing his dog, and – beside the altar – ruining his lawn-mower. 'Now', I fancy the scenario ran, 'I'm going to finish your no-good life, you ne'er-do-well. Say your last prayers and give up the ghost.' Following which the gun fired a blank, and Batty surreptitiously smeared ketchup from a concealed bottle over his robe and face. A third crony sold the photos to the *News of the World* for an undisclosed sum.

It was this charming imbecile who regularly gave me three bisques and still beat me. Tonight, thinking intermittently of Blanche Afanasian's open lips and warm, firm bosom, I was losing more heavily than usual. The last point of all was controversial, and our marker, Noël St James, remained nonplussed, trying to work out who had won it by repeating aloud what had happened. 'Batty as striker-out, playing for a short chase, forced very hard for the dedans. The ball grazed the server's racquet and took a deflection to the bandeau above the dedans; it then returned over the net without touching the floor on the service side, and dropped on

the floor on the hazard side. Now, if David definitely struck the ball when he tried to stop the force with a volley, the return was good, but I don't see that he did make a definite strike.'

Mesurier from the dedans heard this and put his oar in. 'Law 12 says the return is not good if the ball, having passed the net, comes back and drops on the side from which it was struck, unless it touched a gallery-post or anything fixed or lying in an opening on that side of the court opposed to the striker.'

Batty, bored by rules, had left the Court to change and I followed him, having conceded by a nod and a bredouille.

We chaffed each other while changing, and left together, I to my Accord, he to his Porsche. There was a girl in his passenger seat; I waved 'Lizzie!' but a second impulse drove me to the car, and there I saw as if in trance not Lizzie at all, but Blanche Afanasian! Batty, who might well have heard that Blanche belonged to one of my tutor groups, powered off with her. What does Lizzie know? What does Lizzie care? How long has McMan known Blanche and – worse still – how intimately? It's not a matter that one can mention to him, to Blanche, or to Sophie. I composed a letter to an agony aunt:

'Dear Flossie. I am infatuated with one of my students, whom I have been too tongue-tied to approach. Meanwhile my best friend, also married with two young children, has seduced her without telling me of his intentions. What should I do?' Reply 'Dear Heartsore, West Hartlepool, I accept this could be a severe test of your friendship, but since the young lady in question is clearly available, I suggest you grab an equal piece of skirt without letting your best friend know. Only thus can honour be salved. Your ever loving Flossie.' Or words to that effect.

I tried to make passionate love to Sophie that night, but she complained of being dog-tired, and over her soft, deeply-breathing body, I faced the endless patterns of a professional masseur, whose ministrations might be viewed as – purely professional.

18

Next day was Saturday, when Tithe Barn Antiques would presumably experience their busiest day, as bargain hunters spread their motorised tentacles across the Home Counties. I resolved to become one of their number, and donned a casual outfit, with a suede jacket in the back of the car in case the weather turned chillier. 'The Pursuit of Rose Napcott' might have been entered in my diary if I had ever been so incautious as to start one. What foolish desire for notoriety impels an otherwise sane individual to maintain incriminating evidence for blackmailers, journalists, and biographers?

Had Rose kept any of the letters I had written her? How many had I written: three? four? It was after we parted that I stopped writing to women, or at least writing down dates and names, so that if I were confronted with one, with irrefragable evidence of its authenticity, I could always claim it was written to someone else, at a different time. But it would still be better if I knew they had been torn up.

'I'm going to see Yukič about trying to get out of that Seminar in Glasgow next month', I said, as I kissed Sophie on the cheek after breakfast. And that of course – if you wanted to know – was quite true, except that I was going to ask Yukič on Monday morning. Why did I have to spend precious days in gloomy Glasgow when I could have been devoting my free afternoons to Blanche Afanasian in the Crowne Plaza or the Post House at Impington?

Newport High Street, somnolent in gusts of leafladen winds, seemed like one of those streets in Nile Delta towns which conceal infinitely more than they reveal. Would Rose have put on her black panties and bra? Would she have gazed in the mirror at her curves before applying lipstick? Would she have stroked her sides and shoulders in awareness of her own sensuality? And would Napcott, still partly in darkness with the curtains not yet fully opened, have watched her naked back sway and straighten and sway again as she hooked her bra tight?

I stopped casually at the Tithe Barn Antiques window, a copper warming-pan glinting at me above a distressed sideboard. No sign of Rose. No sign of Victor Napcott. I opened the door and the familiar bell jangled.

At length Napcott emerged, but seemed not to recognise me. I started up.

'Mr Napcott. Morning. Glad you could come to dinner. Have you by any chance a spyi-blugs – one of those water-jugs used by Tibetan monks to rinse their hands and mouth after meals?'

His mind groped in vast space: two vacua.

'Whatsat?'

'Do you have one of those ancient wind-up gramophones with a horn and a little dog?'

'We don't touch gramophones,' relied our hero, who regularly savours in bed the profuse, sleek flesh of my bud rose.

'Anything at the back? I don't see anything here that I'm particularly looking for.'

He peered at me helplessly like a pimp incapable of realising what a client sees in his protegée. The long hairs in his nostrils stretched out, waggling and waving gently like strands attached to the seabed.

I pushed past his clock-shells, emptied of horological meaning. Rose was in the garden at the back. My brain was a silly pendulum: how, when, how, when… I could not take my eye off her body as she polished a large mahogany table in the open air, rapt in her manual work, her lustrous brown hair untidy from exertion and a breeze. But I had to go back through the shop, bid Napcott farewell, or risk spoiling everything. After all, had he resolved not to invite her, had he merely forgotten to invite her, or had she turned the invitation down?

I made my way down the High Street, and bought a *Saffron Walden Weekly News* in the vain hope that it might contain a portrait of Rose, who had so recently taunted my body with her once-only willingness, who had so long ago lain with me on her father's hearthrug in the crackling firelight.

An undergraduate called Simbold had once explained to me through his pincushion of acne that my attraction towards Rose produced the hormone norepinephrine in my nerve endings and adrenal glands. Combined with dopamine, this hormone created euphoria, a quickening of the pulse, a need to talk, and a feeling of desperate aggression overcoming shyness. Advances could be made.

I could pursue Rose through the fire and water prescribed by Sarastro for Tamino, but if Pamina refused to undergo the same tests in the same spirit, would not my purification be in vain?

At the time when Rose and I were making such infrequent love, I had consoled myself for part of the time with sex magazines, and for part of the time with the thirteenth-century poem *The Romance of the Rose*, seeing in the allegory of courtly love my passion for my own Rose reflected. A woman's strangest power is nevertheless in her hours and days away, when your memory of her warm, melting meeting flesh intensifies without the danger of anti-climax. At the same time I dipped into the rabid obscenities of Rabelais, and was torn between the fantastic worlds of eros and agape. There is something to be said for achieving the right balance, if only anyone had ever discovered the right balance. The synchronicity of erection between my cock and Rose's nipples seemed at one time a demonstration of eros, like the anagrammatic summation of her name, but whenever I thought about her later on, I remembered a kind of holy living and holy dying full of sacramental power, like the Mithraic ritual of slaying a bull. I was destined to thrust my pricking rapier inside her, following which she would sleep, and I too would then sleep, the rite concluded. We dispensed with foreplay, that grace before eating, and tore at each other's arms and legs like praying mantises for whom sex and death are wholly intertwined.

But there is an adolescent experimentation, where the identity of the partners (and perhaps even their gender) is less interesting than the exploring of new sensations for their own sake.

In adolescence one is never sure how much of one's sexual involvement is due to the need to experiment, and how much is due to affection. In Rose's case I thought I was using her as an outlet for simple periodic lust, whereas it is now clear I felt a true and lasting affection for her. You either live with a woman like that, or you marry her. I had idiotically done neither, and now I was paying the price in a kind of remorse and longing.

She had obviously felt that I was a ripe case for testing her charms, and still thought that now. She had proved that her power over me had not vanished; it had presumably not even diminished. And for her, that knowledge was enough. She could go back to her long-haired nostrilled Napcott in the certain knowledge that I, a randy dog, was barking and leaving traces below her window in the hope of attracting the bitch above. And that was all I could expect.

❦ 19 ❦

So what I did next was what I had always done in the presence of a brick wall straight ahead. Instead of hitting my head against it, or veering off with random hussies pacing Lion Yard, with drug-pushers, or dozy alcoholics, I pattered up the open steps, bear-protected, to the Sedgwick Museum, reassuring in the stupendous age of its fossils.

As a boy at Swavesey Village College, I had been a member of a school outing with Mr Towell to the Sedgwick, with its towering skeletons of dinosaurs, and its delicately chipped stone tools of prehistoric man so much lovelier than our own massive spades, forks, rakes and hoes. I had wanted desperately to be a Stone Age man with his freedom to hunt and fish, his animal-hide clothes even smellier than Tom Sawyer's or Huck Finn's, and his obvious disdain for washing every day.

In later life I had become entranced by the thought of the Cam Valley tropical jungle as it was during the Pleistocene 120,000 years ago. My contemporaries looked at pictures of hippos and rhinos in Africa, or went to London Zoo. I knew that during the Ipswichian phase of the last Interglacial Age they had wandered across the hot humid wetlands among spotted hyenas, lions, bison, aurochs, brown bears, and elephants. For others, the Sedgwick was a museum of dead bone, mute stone; for me, it breathed anger, danger, fear and blood as lionesses stalked their game across the savannah between Toft and Barrington. I sniffed the stench of rotting carcasses, just as the jackals had done.

Distress over leaving a girl-friend loses its pang, born of jealousy and mocked pride, in surroundings where a millennium is a brief interlude between two others. A neat demonstration of adzes from first to last can span a hundred thousand years, and I? I shall be lucky to live another sixty years from the moment of closing the heavy wooden door behind, emerging on to Downing Street, a potentially wiser, more balanced man. Until I see the next tight skirt.

I lunched at the Graduate Centre, and there I bumped into Batty McMan again. The question was irresistible, as I passed his table, where he was eating with three fellows I didn't know. 'Saw you leave Grange Road with one of my group, Afanasian,' I said.

'That's right. She's lodging with us, didn't you know?'

Lodging? Could Lizzie really put up with the copper-haired Armenian beauty, scented and exotic, alluring Batty every moment that Lizzie's back was turned? I nodded at the other three fellows and carried on to a table for those who hadn't reserved.

I glowed with renewed confidence. This was not a secret liaison: Blanche was not tied to this hoaxer by any passion. But then, if I were to entangle her, Batty would be sure to find out, then Lizzie, then Sophie's circle, then, by that curious process I had named the Duchess of Berwick ploy (after *Lady Windermere's Fan*), finally Sophie herself. She clearly realised that my loyalty was to her, but women are remarkable prickly about such matters, sometimes damned intransigent and nothing but problems would arise.

So the best method of securing secrecy would be to remove Blanche from a house where I was well-known to a house where I was unknown. I could righteously refer to Batty's rapscallion history before he'd married Lizzie and, for all I knew, equally scandalous behaviour thereafter.

I too had taken advantage of Sophie's absence at the shops to have sex with a middle-aged chambermaid during my honeymoon, but that was a simple assurance as to my stamina, and the woman – surprised though she might have been by my theatrical raptures above her parted legs – seemed completely gratified by the compliment and the large tip placed discreetly in her left shoe while she was rearranging her hair with Sophie's silver brush.

Batty used disguises like Errol Flynn, Roger Moore, and oddly enough Alf Garnett to endow his premarital adventures with that frisson belonging to his favourite John Buchan era, when men were rugged explorers and women petite drudges. He was once found in bed with a daughter of the Master of Caius: she was wearing black rubber from a sex shop (presumably brought along by Batty) and he had disrobed from a World War I aviator's costume hired from the Festival Theatre. Macho Biggles meets Kinky Worrals. The whole affair was hushed up and, so far from suffering any great punishment for being nabbed *in flagrante delicto*, Batty exacted some nebulous form of blackmail from the Master, according to Stibbers Calthrop, my informant, not wholly unconnected with jeroboams of Moët et Chandon champagne.

✿ 20 ✿

One of the prices exacted from a Lecturer in Arabic Literature in these days of restricting budgets and dire cuts is to attend one or more of the various seminars, courses, and conferences which give an impression that in some real sense a species of scholarship is moving – at a more or less gratifying pace – forward. Some of us are actually expected to organise such confabulations, or deliver papers, or host parties, or chair sessions: there is no end to the responsibilities with which the unwary young scholar can be ensnared in the belief that somehow getting the right number of slides in a lantern-lecture viewer will enhance his chance of a Chair at Dundee or Wollongong.

I have no such heady ambitions: at Cambridge you have little or no chance of a Chair if your pedagogical origins can be traced back to Swavesey Village College. But I was still embroiled as a matter of custom in the annual Seminar on Modern Arabic Literature held in rotation between an American city (last year Pittsburgh), an Arab city (next year Tunis), and a European city (this year Glasgow). This arrangement ensures that we shall all get expenses-paid trips regularly to the U.S.A. and the Arab World, and that our colleagues overseas regularly visit us.

I had been asked to give a paper this year for the first time, and chose the theme of 'Time and Timelessness in the Novels of Naguib Mahfouz.' Last year there had been a paper on 'Place and Placelessness in the Writings of Tayib Salih,' and 'Fear and Fearlessness in the Work of Fathi Ghanam' and I felt that my title would touch a chord. I could always read Naguib's *Children of Gebelawi* in the train north, and make enough notes to embroider into a seamless cloak, or whatever. Sam Glotz, the Organiser, would want a text to publish, but I could fob him off with the recent deaths in the family and offer something later on.

Who else would be there? Haya al-Hamid, for one, a liberated Moroccan lady who had lived for several years with the titan of Moroccan poetry, Zaid al-Maqlawi. She had

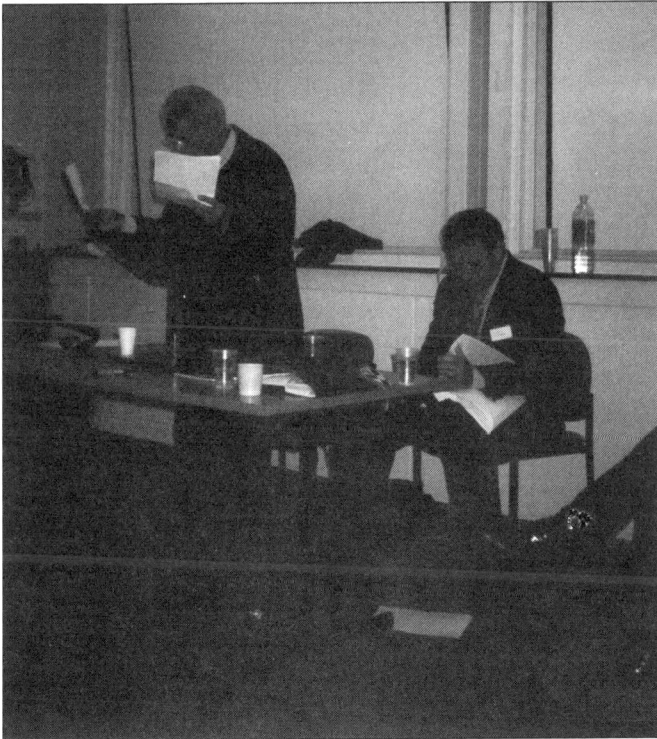

threatened to bring Zaid along each year, but this year he was in Britain anyway on a tour arranged by the Moroccan Embassy, and his bass tones, familiar from tapes and records, would thunder across the university lecture-hall, obliterating any timid whispering. We were all afraid of Zaid al-Maqlawi.

اليمن: تفتيش استفزازي لمقبل وجار الله في مطار صنعاء

صنعاء: حسين الجرياني

قال الحزب الاشتراكي اليمني المعارض ان اثنين من زعمائه تعرضا لمضايقات من سلطات مطار صنعاء الدولي اول من امس. واضاف بيان صدر عن مسؤول في المكتب السياسي «ان علي صالح عباد الامين العام للحزب وجار الله عمر عضو المكتب السياسي ووزير الثقافة الاسبق قد جرى تأخيرهما لحوالى ساعة عند وصولهما مساء الجمعة الماضي من خارج اليمن. واشار البيان الى ان عملية التأخير هذه تمت تحت ذريعة ان بحوزتهما كتبا وانه لا يمكن خروجهما من المطار ومعهما هذه الكتب الا بتصريح من مندوب وزارة الثقافة والسياحة. واوضح ان مقبل وجار الله قد اخضعا لتفتيش بطريقة وصفت بانها استفزازية ولم يسمح لهما بالخروج من المطار بصورة اعتيادية وان ذلك التأخير الاستفزازي المتعمد لقادة «الاشتراكي» بغرض الاستفزاز

والمضايقات، حسب تعبير المسؤول الاشتراكي.

وعلى صعيد الاعتقالات التي شهدتها مدينة جعار بمحافظة ابين عبر المكتب السياسي للحزب الاشتراكي في بيان له امس بهذا الخصوص عن اسفه لهذه الاجراءات التي وصفها بالمخالفة للدستور.

واورد بيان المكتب السياسي اسماء من اعتقلوا من كوادره في محافظة ابين، وعددهم 16 شخصا وهم حسين عوض عبد القوي عضو اللجنة المركزية سكرتير منظمة الاشتراكي بمحافظة ابين، عامر الصدري، علي دهس، حسين سعيد سالم سكرتير منظمة الاشتراكي في مديرية جعار، محمد ابو بكر هندي، محمد سعيد، سالم عبد الله، عبد الله حسين محمد، عوض ثابت عوض، محمد حازم عبد الرب، علي حيدرة النقي، سالم صالح الخيال، عبد الرحمن الشهلي، حسين فضل شتم، سيف سالم محسن، فايز احمد الهامل.

Then there was Sam Glotz, as was, who called himself Roderick Findlay since the Arab Boycott of Israel. We all knew him as Sam, and his wife Golda made an unambiguous figure as Jewish Cookery expert on cable television. I was looking forward to seeing Burgess Doyle from Khartoum, Neil and Jamila Strutt from Damascus, and the stringy, pedantic Fitzstephen Leggate from Oxford. I dreaded the loud contingent from the States, headed by the redoubtable enemies Olithorn from Yale and Harbick from Princeton. Whether they were arguing about Yusuf Idris or Ghassan Kanafani they ended up like the tough guys in any favourite Hollywood Western, eyeballing each other from a very short distance and once had in fact come to blows over a disputed interpretation of Abdul Malik's *Song of the Earth*. I have always been mildly gratified that such a supposedly innocent field could produce such heavy and violent turnips.

Sam had at least made sure that if Harbick chaired one session, Olithorn would chair the next; and that neutrals such as the retired Duff from Manchester and the innocuous Doyle would chair the first and last. I didn't think much of such pseudo-diplomacy, for animosities would emerge in grilles and dedans if not on the service side or hazard side of the court.

I was hoping to be able to make time alone with the sultry if acid-tongued Haya, who once told an enthralled press conference in San Diego that she had modelled her life on that of the emancipated Bulgarian poetess Elizaveta Bagryana. Her collected poems, *The Eternal and the Stars*, imitate both title and content of the immortal Bagryana, who admitted to having 'a husband in every country.' Haya's roving eye had not yet lighted on me, though I had seen a photograph of her, black eyes fixed hypnotically on the camera, a cigarette in a holder tilted at an angle suited to display her fat rings on plump fingers; she was running to that fat which Arabs seek in emulation of worshippers of Hathor, Pharaonic sacred cow.

Zaid by contrast was running to thinness, with a trim Mephistophelean beard and a tiny, elegant moustache. He reminded me of a tortoise concealed in the lazy carapace of Haya. He was giving a press conference in Arabic to various journalists representing the Arabic press in Britain, and a tape-recorder hummed in the background. 'What is your opinion of the Palestine struggle?' I heard. 'How can the role of the Arab writer today be used to assist the working classes?' And from a woman in a head-scarf and dark glasses: 'Do you attempt to correct the distorted view of women in Arab society through your poetry?' It was clear that, as always in Arab countries, the questioner was posing problems that affected the questioner, in such a manner as to predicate the answer. Nobody asked Zaid about the devious processes by which he dredged words and images from the subterranean passages of his soul. Yes, he was a libertine, an atheist, a man devoted to the immediate satisfaction of desire. But beyond all this he listened to what the fickle muse was saying; with his eyes closed, he deliberately watched the songstress weaving patterns that he could use as a structure for the heated words, planned or random, that jostled and jetstreamed in his cauldron of memory. I tried to follow the veiled movements of Haya al-Hamid's breasts but her long dress was too conventionally voluminous to offer more than a hint of the pendulous breasts that lay beneath Zaid each night.

'Quitregard, isn't it?' enquired the wintry lips of Leggate, many years my senior. 'Dr Leggate, I hope to hear your paper tomorrow. Are you staying at the Albany?' 'Mrs Leggate has gone to Loch Lomond. I told her it's much too cold at this time of year, but you know what women are.'

'Excuse me. Burgess! Haven't seen you since Shemlan! I knew you were coming. How are you?'

'Pretty depressed about teaching Arabic literature in Sudan, when most people haven't got enough to eat, never mind enough to read. I feel I shouldn't be there, eating their food. What do they need with Tawfiq al-Hakim and Jibran Jibran? Do you know Jeremy? We're together. He's from London, but he's teaching English in Omdurman.'

'Excuse me.'

I had just seen an extraordinary vision, and left Burgess Doyle and his friend Jeremy to head nonchalantly towards it. The vision was Julia Baneath, a near contemporary of mine at Cambridge. She had been at Newnham while I was at King's, and we had attended a series of special lectures together, and drank at the pubs around Silver Street bridge. Then we had spent a marvellous weekend together at Aldeburgh, pretending we were Peter Grimes and Ellen Orford. There was no concert at the Maltings, so the barn gaped, gaunt and spurious, bereft of its resounding cello, the madcap bicycle of Albert Herring, the agonised rape of Lucretia. Julia had the most unearthly smile, radiant, Ariel, Puck, Ophelia, and it is that smile I see whenever I hear a concert from Snape, or whenever I enter one of the old barns at Swavesey. I was twenty and she would have been about nineteen, so now twenty-seven. Then she had been incensed by Thatcherism but desolated by the brutality and incompetence, the corruption and anti-intellectual militarism of Saddam Hussein. Now she was wearing a Greenpeace badge and her handsome Scottish features, once softened by milder East Anglian summers, had retreated into their weatherbeaten mould that I recalled so well.

'What are you *doing*, Julia?'

She did not accept my proffered hand, but gave me that same waxen, ethereal smile that bore in it suffering and patience, like the smile of Beauty in Cocteau's *Beauty and the Beast.*

'I didn't take my Oriental Languages degree, you remember,' she said, her soft Scottish accent slightly modulated by the Newnham years. No, I hadn't remembered anything of the sort. I was in my third year at King's while she was still a fresher, and I had left for pastures new before she would have been due to graduate.

'After you left I switched to English, and took a third. Then I did library science at Loughborough and I've been at the Mitchell and the Stirling ever since.'

'And the Greenpeace badge?'

'I've no party. With nuclear holocausts hanging over us, there's only one party to belong to. The human party, the race to survive in spite of governments and politicians.'

'The Green Party?'

'A waste of time, Davie.' I noted with alacrity the incipient friendship denoted by the use of my name, as she used to say it during bouts of lovemaking. 'Nobody outside the narrow system of self-interests is ever going to gain power. The only way is to throw bombs.'

I laughed at this tall, blue-eyed brunette who had guided our bodies together throughout two starlit nights on the Suffolk coast, in a hotel room rented by Mr and Mrs Quitregard.

Old Duff, once Professor of Arabic at Manchester, patted me on the shoulder. 'Ah, Dolethorpe,' he grinned, complacently. 'No, sir, Quitregard, from Cambridge.' 'Quite so,' mumbled Duff, and mooned off to pat Harbick on the shoulder, and call him Olithorn.

'Don't you think we should retire somewhere for lunch, Julia?'

'It's a bit early for lunch.'

'You can show me something of your lovely Glasgow, if the rain keeps off.'

'Where are you staying?'

'Down the hill, at Balsimer's Hotel, in Sauchiehall Street. We can go back there for a few minutes. But they don't serve lunch.'

We were clearly both relieved to leave the incestuous atmosphere of a room where nattering and snapping over views of Muhammad Taimur or his brother Mahmud can seem as world-shaking as a dispute over bacon-rind can seem to two starlings.

'Do you know why I can't go back to Cambridge?' said Julia as we sped down the path from the University towards Kelvin Way. The wind swirled in her scintillating brown hair.

'No,' I replied, hoping to draw her out on the missing years since I had gone abroad.

'Because I once heard a don saying at a party and I quote: I'm sure there have been acceptable books in English since the thirteenth century, but somehow I have always felt, and correct me if I'm wrong, that since the *Ancrene Riwle* and the *Ayenbite of Inwyt*, it's all been a matter of marking time.'

We giggled helplessly, all the way to my hotel. I collected my key and we went up to my room on the first floor, beside a great metal contraption that promised tea, coffee, chocolate, Bovril, Horlicks and Chicken Soup for 50p each. I inserted a 50p-piece, pulled a lever, and a little metal tin of concentrated dust popped down a chute. I opened the container, shook the powder into a plastic cup, and added boiling-hot water. 'Chicken Soup?' I said. 'All right,' said Julia, still smiling: did she know that the don had been satirising his foes, and did it matter if the joke was not on the don but on her?

We took our plastic cups inside, and I sat on the bed. She wore a blue coat over her stylish blue suit. The trousers, I noted, were flecked with mud.

'Julia, I've until tomorrow when I don't have to turn up at the Seminar. Will you stay with me, as it used to be?'

She looked at me steadily, as if weighing my soul at the Gates of Heaven.

'Have you time off?'

She answered, 'I've today as my weekly day off, and I've tomorrow covering the event for the *Glasgow Herald*.'

'Perfect. Do you want lunch?' Question expecting the answer no.

'That's what I was hoping you'd say. And I can show you my Glasgow in the afternoon.'

'How do you know I'm a stranger here?'

'I couldna see Davie Quitregard making many special journeys to see the Pride o' the Clyde,' with tongue in cheek. Of course she was right. I had fallen in love with Julia Baneath because she was wiser than I by several light years: a wisdom that came from a peasant instinct, I suppose, or from native shrewdness allied to a splendidly selective education allied to a sense of humour and a power of discrimination between right and wrong that was more than religious or moral but in some tragic way Antigonean. I could see her envenom Creon with her poisoned tongue not because she had any great store of malice in her, but because of her towering righteousness. She could have stood in for the Statue of Liberty at the entrance to the Clyde. There are some characters who are convinced they are right but are actually wrong, like Napoleon, Hitler, Marx, Mussolini and Mao. There are others who are convinced they are right and are actually right, like Galileo, Schweitzer, Leonardo and Confucius. Julia Baneath was the only denizen of the latter category I had ever met, and I had been instantly won over to all her causes: to the economic democracy of C.H. Douglas, to the mime of Marcel Marceau, the plight of the Xingu Indians of Brazil and the need to protect all rain forests, and to love the whale and to hate the despicable whaling (and sealing) industry. She daily opened *The Guardian* for news of mighty victories; daily she flagged as the defeats were made known; daily she revived her energies to attend rallies, and to stick stamps on envelopes addressed to policy-makers, world leaders, or to men in the street who

enquired for free pamphlets. Julia had never married; she espoused instead the cause of Afghani women under the Taliban and became one of them for a weekend in Trafalgar Square, returning home to pursue the struggle for a saner world by writing and disseminating literature to those who were already converted, would never be converted, or sat uncomfortably on the fence, guiltily perhaps, or perhaps awaiting evidence that would prove decisive. Julia herself needed no exhortation. Reasonably, and without noticeable rancour, she went out on cold winter nights to ill-attended meetings, sitting among cranks who thumped desks in chilly primary schools, and among tired housewives knitting during repetitious speeches. And why should the speeches not be repeated if what they said was right? Julia repeated herself to all those with whom she came into contact, not because she was dull, panicky or cranky but because she was expending her precious, limited hours in trying to turn the inevitable tide of intolerance, terrorism, war, commercialism, degradation. Her masters called the motorways and spreading factories 'progressive,' so Julia they dismissed as 'retrogressive.' Doggedly and sensibly aware that money to be made was on the other side, contaminating food and adding lead to petrol, Julia identified with the poor and starving in Ethiopia and Glasgow; she organised sponsorship for sickly children in Sudan, Colombia and war-torn Somalia.

We finished our chicken soup, and Julia quickly rose from my single bed without taking off her blue coat. She took my plastic cup too, and threw both into the basket, then opened the door.

'Dark comes early in Glasgow,' she said lightly. 'I want to show you my city while we've time.' I tried to catch her to hold her arm while we were still private upstairs, but she had run on ahead down the stairs, while I paused to hand over my room-key.

We turned right down Sauchiehall Street, and the drizzle started. I tried to hold Julia's hand, but she kept constantly pointing out what I should notice, and we were being separated by so many Glaswegians with black umbrellas that I thought of it then and think of it still as the City of Crows. At the top of North Street she stopped and pointed down to the Mitchell Library on the right-hand side. Below us roared

endless streams of traffic on the motorway that had turned Glasgow into an appendix to long-haul traffic routes. No by-pass for this commercial centre: just crack open the faint heart of Scotland's metropolis and let the blood run out in all directions. Glasgow took my breath away: a Bedlam for architects who have been struck off the register. Abandon hope, all ye who enter here, for the planners have abandoned all their principles and integrated views. How could my Julia tolerate this inextricable welter of contradictory views: the Gothic and the Art Deco, the 'Greek' of Thomson, and the baroque? Outside my hotel room I had stared in dismay at the dirt-grey bricks and uneven windows opposite; now, traipsing along Berkeley Street and Bath Street with their fake English names and their mangled architectural aspirations, I felt as though the buildings were trying to assault me; scaffoldings threatened to trip me up, blind me with struts, crush me with toppling pails or thudding masonry; toothless gaps of demolished shops and houses leered at me. 'Go home,' they said, 'until we have decided what we are to be. And when we are that, we shall be ugly, and pulled down again to make way for even more forlorn wastes and odd façades with odder rears.'

We took a greasy lunch in the only café open near the Cathedral. Down the hill from Provand's Lordship we found a ruined red-brick warehouse, its immense yard ten-feet high in rubble. BR TISH RAILWAY was its age-worn inscription, and the missing vowel I silently replaced with U.

Julia was undismayed, gaily showing me a mort-safe in the Necropolis, intended to hinder body-snatchers in their gruesome trade, and comparing the Clyde Embankment at Broomielaw with a picture of the Neva Embankment in St Petersburg. 'Do you not like George Street?' 'Do you not like St Vincent Place?'

I was noncommittal with a view to seducing Julia that night, but waxed properly enthusiastic at the sight of Stirling's Library in the Royal Exchange, a 1780 mansion with a barrel vault covered by a coffered ceiling and illuminated by great chandeliers. Now a branch of Glasgow District Libraries, who employ Julia, the Stirling is open to the world, and here I felt that Glasgow had at last managed to leave well alone.

'Now before you leave you can see the Burrell Collection and the City Art Gallery,' admonished Julia as courier. 'If you've a free evening you're to go to the Citizens' Theatre.'

'Where do you live, Julia?'

'It's out of the centre.'

'I've a free evening. Do you want to go to the Citizens'?'

'It's *The Plough and the Stars*. I've seen it. Have you no sherry party at the Seminar?'

'Come back to the hotel.'

'Just for an hour. I've to go back to cook the dinner.'

She still did not take my hand, and we must have looked like strangers, if any passing Glasgow gudewife had chosen to consider us.

'I'm surprised, after Lebanon and Cairo, that you don't want to leave Cambridge, Davie.'

I was puzzled by this conversational ploy, but politely maintained the tone, 'Well, you know what Lytton Strachey said, "Cambridge is the only place I never want to leave, though I suffer more there than anywhere else".'

'If you lived in Glasgow, you'd suffer more here than anywhere else. The people have moved out of the East End. There were 150,000 there in 1961, and only fifty thousand now.' She seemed angrily resigned, perhaps resentful of my southern ignorance of inner-city drug abuse and vandalism.

'Is there no hope then, Julia?'

'I'm part of the Glasgow Eastern Area Renewal Project, trying to talk to people in my spare time to see what they want.'

'And what do they want?'

She laughed hollowly. ' "A hoose wi' a front door, a back door, and mebbe a bi' o' gairden." They might as well ask for a mansion in Upper Phillimore Gardens.' That was where an aunt of hers had spent one never-to-be-forgotten summer before being widowed and turned out of Kensington following a legal wrangle.

'Nothing works because everybody is a planner amateur or professional, and the plans contradict each other, district by district, and year by year. The Scottish Parliament says one thing, then the Strathclyde Region vetoes that, then the Glasgow District Council offers another suggestion, and the Scottish Parliament vetoes that.'

'And the drunks? Do they get worse?'

'The few who survive get worse. You've seen the Glasgow alkies on street corners: they're as much part of life here as the ones by the Embankment are in London. But then there's the hard lads who are on meths. Below them are the desperate ones, drinking hair lacquer mixed with lemonade. I saw four of them, like bridge-players, seated around a fire of rubbish on a waste-tip last night. The flames were seeking out the light in their faces, but I saw only the grey and black of shadows and darkness escaping the illumination. They forget the names of their friends, and then their own. You find them lying in doorways, in the morning. The heroin is much worse: they kill for heroin.'

I kept quiet because Julia's face, large and full-fleshed, its aggressive jaw at odds with generous lips and gentle eyes, had gone pale, as her voice had sharpened. What I represented at that moment, to Julia, was the dreamlike view of King's Chapel from West Road, punting after a May Ball to Grantchester, the riotous, bibulous hilarity of a college feast, the expensive quiet of the new Robinson College library, closed to outsiders.

At every step in her sensible shoes she silently tapped out, ar, son, van, dal, is, m, tu, ber, cu, lo, sis, al, co, hol, is, m, he, ro, in, de, mo, li, tion. How could she discuss it with me? Would I, could I, ever understand?

'What is to be done?' I asked her, after a decent interval. But she considered me past redemption.

'Most of the time nobody talks about Camlachie or Calton or Shettleston or Tollcross, and you're on holiday, Davie, so I'm to change the subject.'

'Not on my account, Julia. You know we shared everything, that weekend at Aldeburgh.'

'Why did you invite me to Aldeburgh, that time? Was it because you wanted to share my life with me?'

'Of course it was.' Her shoulder-bag hit me, accidentally I think, and she moved closer to the dingy shops and offices on Sauchiehall Street. We were nearly back at the hotel. The rain began again, but she was ready for it with scarf and umbrella, which I offered to hold for her. 'I'll not need your help,' she said, ambiguously.

The receptionist gave me my key with eyes averted to give me the impression that he was not prying.

'Coffee if it's drinkable,' she commanded, as we stopped by the drinks machine near my door. An Italian woman emerged from the door opposite, scolding her man for losing something like a pin. Her anguished 'perduuuuto' echoed down the passageway and down the stairs.

I opened the door, thankful that Julia was not about to make an italianate scene. She took off her coat and scarf, then her wet trousers, her tights, and her panties. Then her jacket. She wore a neat pink blouse with a brooch: and was naked from the hips down. She sat on the bed, then raised her knees up to her chin, exposing her mass of dark pubic hair.

I left the room to spurt hot water into two cups, each with their dark brown third-grade coffee powder. She had remained in the same position, looking into a mental distance between her knees and the door, but swivelled her head to look into the mirror flecked with fly-dirt.

'You can watch me, Davie,' she said slowly, as her fingers descended to her springy hair, and made a rhythmic rubbing motion, followed by a sucking sound. I knelt before her and rested my head on her inner thigh, letting my tongue dart within. We were sufficiently experienced, in those far-off Aldeburgh hours, not to be inhibited by what 'society might think,' but Julia had lost little of her voluptuary's power, and I, like all men, found the conquest of an unfamiliar or half-forgotten woman more tantalisingly exciting than the routine embraces of my own wife. But Julia was less adroit than Sophie with her lips and tongue, and I withdrew my cock once from her mouth because she hurt. 'Soft, soft,' I said, but withdrew again before orgasm in order to fuck her. Instead she rubbed the hard long cock until I spurted across her legs and on the carpet, while penetrating her mouth with my darting tongue. Matter-of-factly she rubbed the semen off her legs with two tissues from her shoulder-bag. She was no romantic. She clicked her shoulder-bag shut and dressed again.

'You're not going?'

'Why not? Haven't we met again, as you wanted?'

'I wanted to stay with you.'

'I told you. I've to get the dinner.'

'Can I see you again tomorrow?'

'There are plenty of girls in Glasgow, Davie. Little Tamara Ransome will be at the Seminar tomorrow. I've told her all about you.'

'You've what?'

'I've told her what a promising young scholar you are. She likes Ansari, and she's doing Persian as well as Arabic so she might have some ideas about Ansari's works in Persian.'

Her eyes were somnolent, and she lay on the bed beside me, fully dressed, but still would not take my hand in token of an affection not explicitly sexual.

I could hardly discuss a totally unknown woman's prowess immediately after sex with Julia, but she in mock-innocence chose not to see that, and continued to tell me about the young Scottish Arabists in Glasgow for the Seminar. It was true; I knew only the English and a few of the Arab contingent and two or three of the Americans.

'Run along to your sherry party,' she said, rising decisively and patting me on the knee. She was treating me just like a friendly don's wife would treat an undergraduate.

'Just a minute,' I said, almost annoyed by her dismissive attitude. 'Tell me what you've been doing since we last met.'

'It will only take a minute,' she said, seeming slyly to indicate I had been condescending in my turn. 'You know that I abandoned Arabic when I found out rather late about the arms the British had been supplying to Saddam. Or was it that I wasn't good enough at Arabic and was glad of any excuse? Well, in any case, I thought English would be less fraught with broken glass and broken plurals, and I was right. But I still found to my growing alarm that English writers had never

touched the real problem. Oh, I know Leavis told us about the great tradition, and McCabe realised that there was something in structuralism so had to be thrown out – to Scotland as it happened. But Brewer was hemmed in by the whole irrelevance of medievalism and the Prynneites were so precious and slim-talented that they actually succeeded in killing off the Cambridge Poetry Society altogether for a time. I suppose it was only Steiner who made 'English' seem a proper study because he took the English out of it, and gave us back Dante and Celan.'

She was glancing sidelong at me during much of this, as if challenging me to detect which of her opinions were first-hand, or second-hand, or third-. I gave nothing away: I waited.

She was making up her mind how much to say. I was sure of her wisdom, but less convinced of her truthfulness. She had been at Cambridge, where distinct levels of truth have been investigated and described by Wittgenstein, Bronowski, Leavis, and Richards, to say nothing of the wider divagations of Steiner, to whom Julia had alluded. Empson may have enumerated seven types of ambiguity, but Julia had been familiar with at least twice that figure, and may have invented a few kinds herself. Sparring with Arabic for a year or two would have helped, too, because there is no more intriguingly deceptive narrative than the *Thousand and One Nights*, told by a woman, one might add, were it not for the fact that the book was invented by a man. Or by several. Julia was another Shahrazad, just like Rose Calder or Blanche de l'Orient.

After an eternity, as the autumnal evening perceptibly advanced its cloak around us, she continued.

'I didn't want to teach English to freckled adolescents with shrieky voices, braces on their teeth, and crushes on teacher. I wanted to find ultimate meaning myself, not pass on to schoolkids my unformed and immature notions of what others took it to be. I read a good deal of philosophy at home in Fife, then I realised I should have to go back to England to make a career for myself. As my mother said, a woman must have a career. My father had left home for a career in Silicon Valley, leaving us behind. We get a card every Christmas. Two Christmases ago it was different. The message was "Love from Edgar and Luellen" – that is, Louise and Ellen but made one name for one woman. He'd married again. A divorce in Reno, and I suppose a new woman in Reno. It's a disposable society.'

'So I had to have a career, and I chose librarianship. They gave me a place at Loughborough and there I qualified and became a chartered librarian, in between weekends protesting outside embassies and army installations. I've demonstrated at detention centres for asylum-seekers like Oakington because you have to care, even if caring is wrong. I've no doubt you call it all wrong, Davie, because you never did give a damn for anything, did you?'

'So you settled down in Glasgow?'

'You mean why did I choose Glasgow or why did I settle down?'

'Why Glasgow, say, instead of Dundee or Edinburgh?'

'You know, Davie, Edinburgh isn't really a problem. It's nothing I can do anything about, too genteel, too English, not risky enough. If you want a challenge in Western Europe, I suppose Glasgow is the place to be. If you had the nerve, you'd come too.'

'Wouldn't your husband mind that?'

She laughed uproariously.

'I'm leaving now, otherwise I'll be too late to make the dinner, and there'll be questions asked. Just remember you're dealing with a hardened jailbird, Davie, when you see me at the Seminar tomorrow.'

She was gone through the door, along the worn carpet so I could hear the diminishing rhythm of her shoes, and down the stairs to the reception desk.

I shivered, then put on my raincoat before crossing the road to an Indian restaurant with an inviting list of tandoori dishes on its menu.

I dreamt again of the Twin Towers, perpendicular still as stolid bookends; then again the first plane crashed into the first tower, obscenely accurate; then again the second plane crashed into the second tower, in slower and slower motion while I screamed a warning into thin air. There I am again, trying to dream the towers safe, the Muslims violent only in their imagination safe themselves far away in their fantastic caverns.

21

The following morning I arrived early at the Seminar, hoping to solve the riddle of Julia's reference to 'a jailbird,' but she wasn't anywhere near the Lecture Hall, and instead Neil Strutt excitedly cornered me, as he had to tell somebody.

Apparently his wife Jamila had been called in to settle an argument about bride-price with a young couple, the woman from the Gulf and the man from Iraq. Neil was worried that if Jamila sided with the Iraqi he would sue her and, as an Iraqi citizen herself, Jamila might be liable to prosecution when she next returned to her family in Baghdad. He was studying at the University of Strathclyde and she was the daughter of a shipping magnate partly resident in Glasgow, and partly in the Gulf. The bridegroom's father had paid the agreed bride-price

يقول عراقيون ان الاحتفالات التي نظمتها الحكومة العراقية بمناسبة عيد ميلاد الرئيس العراقي صدام حسين، الثالث والستين اساءت الى الجهود الرامية لرفع الحظر الدولي المفروض على العراق منذ عشر سنوات.

وقالت مصادر عراقية ان ذلك سيؤثر حتى على مساعي رئيس المجلس الوطني العراقي سعدون حمادي الذي وصل الى عمان امس للمشاركة في المؤتمر 103 لاتحاد البرلمانيين الدولي حيث يعتزم طرح قضية الحظر والمفقودين العراقيين ومناطق حظر الطيران والهجمات الاميركية المتكررة على الاراضي العراقية.

واكدت هذه المصادر التي تعد قريبة من الحكومة العراقية ان احدا لم يستطع منع مثل هذه الاحتفالات حتى لا يفسر طلبه على انه خيانة للرئيس. وتعتبر الحكومة الع اقية اقامة مثا هذه

to the bride's parents when the marriage contract had been signed by the bridegroom and the bride's father. By tradition, the official ceremony uniting man and wife in the eyes of God and Man is only a preliminary to the real marriage, which is postponed until after a purely family ceremony. During the interim, the bride stays under her father's roof and the bridegroom may not even see her, much less touch her. Neil showed me a judgement from an Islamic scholar at Al-Azhar University in Cairo which, roughly recollected, ran 'As soon as the marriage contract has been signed, and the bride-price paid, the man has a legal right to the woman, and vice versa. If they have sexual relations in secret, there is no violation of the divine law. A child born of such relations is a legitimate child of the father, unless he refuses to recognise his paternity, in which case the wife is required to prove her assertion.' In other words, a woman may be forced to have sexual relations after the first contract is signed (even though she had not signed it) and may be divorced before the second contract. Precisely this tragedy had occurred, and because Jamila was known to the divorced bride's mother, she had been brought in to cajole, threaten, bribe or in some other way convince the bridegroom that he would have to make amends to the girl, now deflowered.

'Hiya, folks,' waved rotund Sam Glotz, as he staggered in, a Tweedledeeless Tweedledum.

Clint Olithorn was saying to Burgess Doyle something like: 'Y'know, it's seems toadly impassable, but Harbick is passing through his *second* male menopause.'

Haya al-Hamid floated in wearing a diaphanous pink ballgown covering every part of her but hands and face, and humming almost recognisably a passage from one of Umm Kulthum's more famous songs; I knew that because Umm Kulthum had once publicly smacked her on both cheeks for wrecking a melody, and Haya took permanent revenge by humming from the rival's repertory out of tune whenever there was a lull in any conversation. I wonder: did she hum in bed below the contortions of the great Zaid?

Vanderpoel from Brussels came in chatting to Carl Harbick. The absent-minded Duff entered, with a sheaf of papers precariously lodged under his arm and a small orange book, which he was reading so intently that he tripped over a briefcase standing beside the Swedish delegate Eriksson.

Duff ascended the rostrum and looked over his glasses for a gavel. Disappointed, he rapped with his knuckles, then poured himself a glass of water from a dusty, half-empty decanter.

'Gentlemen, and Shaikha Haya, may I have your attention, please? The first paper today is to be given by Dr Quitregard, on 'Time and Timelessness in the Novels of Naguib Mahfouz.' I listened blankly, half-approvingly, till I realised that they had rescheduled my paper to be first, and I had not been told, because I had missed the celebrations and chat about precedence on the previous evening. I might have known that, as the most junior speaker, I should be called on first, to warm up the audience like any fifth-rate comic at a seaside variety show.

And Julia Baneath now walked into the crowded lecture-hall, took out her notepad and pen, and awaited my every word ... My notes were back at the hotel. My mind was a mesh of unsynchronised cogs, gears, and wheels, not attached to any mental engine.

My mouth quickly opened and shut a few times in a soundless yammer, as if the volume had been removed from a film about a monkey. I wandered almost in a trance to the microphone, recalling only too vividly that more relaxed occasion not so long ago when had I gazed helplessly back at the beatific vision of Blanche Afanasian, her sultry face framed by swirls of copper-fiery hair.

'Abu 'l-'Ala in the *Risalat al-Ghufran*,' I began, tapping the microphone in the hope of delaying by a few seconds my abject exposure to pitiless analysis by my elders and betters, 'exhorts us not to abuse Time, for Allah *is* Time. And indeed according to many Muslim theologians, God is the Author of all the evils for which Time is blamed, so to abuse Time is in effect to abuse God. After all, we read in the *Fusus al-Hikam* that ad-Dahr, or, Time without beginning or end, is a name of Allah ...'

The truth is that I had forgotten to open Naguib Mahfouz's *Children of Gebelawi* in the train north, and since my astonishing meeting with Julia Baneath I had lost all sense of time myself, so that I found myself almost totally unprepared for giving the paper announced. While speaking I considered screaming 'Fire!' to clear the building, then realised that my deception would be discovered at once and my lecture merely postponed. Or I could fall in a dead faint, only to be denounced as a malingerer by the nearest doctor. Or I could guiltily own up to having prepared nothing – but then all these potential employers of mine would class me immediately and irrevocably as unreliable.

So I improvised on aspects of Mustafa Manfaluti, on the relevance of Mahfouz's novels about ancient Egypt, on his time-blur affecting the period of British control and the tyranny of Faruq. I expressed admiration for the novelist's grasp of socio-economic realities as Egyptian women struggled for five decades towards equality in marriage and careers. I considered how eternal yet how transient were the Cairene types explored in *Zuqaq Midaq* and *Khan al-Khalili*. As I drew analogies and pointed up similarities, I began to feel that my audience was making efforts to follow my arguments. As I brought my peroration to a flourishing close, the applause was noticeably louder than that which normally greeted a paper read word by word from the rostrum. Julia, to whom I turned for a sign, was nodding at my ally Strutt, who knew that we had met at Cambridge.

If I had not come through as well as I might have done, at least the sweaty terror of collapse had been dissipated. I found that I had spoken for only twenty of the allotted thirty minutes, and that too was a good sign, for those due to speak later would not now be unduly delayed. Another plus. My bloated bladder needed immediate relief, and it was with some strain that I nodded and smiled to those who looked at me as I made my way up the steps and out of the lecture theatre.

'Where's the Gents?', I enquired of a cleaning lady pushing a trolley. She pointed to a door in shadow beside another door marked JANITOR and I fled in before I disgraced myself on the stairs. When I emerged, Julia was waiting with a sheaf of papers.

'These are the preprints of today's papers and most of tomorrow's, except yours', she said. 'Where's yours?'

'Ah, now that, my dear Julia,' I burbled in relief, 'is a very long story and I shall find a cup of coffee over which to tell it.'

I had a sudden desire to phone home to ask Sophie whether the house at Swavesey, just put on the market, had been sold, but I resisted the urge. Julia was several steps ahead of me.

'Where are we going?'

'You can get a cup of coffee in the Hunterian Museum, on the stairs, and it's a safe bet there'll be none of the Seminar people up there.' Over coffee I noticed the dimples in her cheeks for the first time, for they appeared only when she was smiling and she had not smiled much at our previous encounter. Her diamond ring, glittering in the sudden shafts of sunlight penetrating the semi-darkened room from time to time, reminded me in its occasional gleams of the times we had met at Cambridge and parted, and then in Aldeburgh. I wondered whom she had married, and whether she had children. This was not the place to enquire.

'My mother died very recently, and my father died shortly afterwards, so I have not had the time to devote to my Glasgow paper that I should have liked.'

Also, I should have added, I have not been able to concentrate on much since I first imagined touching Blanche Afanasian's lips: kissing them, tonguing them, letting myself spurt and flood between them. Arabic literature, I was coming to realise, was my paid interval between the gentle pursuit of soft women, and increasingly I was also reading for a vicarious life of sexual contentment which, being sexual, meant a brief encounter of ecstasy and a much longer, often almost unbearable, period of waiting for the next encounter. I understood the haunted abyss of a drug-hunter between one fix and the next. To the outside world I looked entirely normal, and I had no temptations to rape or murder, to bestiality or violence of any kind. But what is a normal man? A Muslim polygamist with four wives? An American monogamist WASP laying as many broads as he can before tying himself down in a febrile marriage soon eclipsed in Nevada? A bowler-hatted insurance clerk commuting afresh daily from Dorking Monumentward, then jaded from Monument Dorkingward?

Julia was silently sipping coffee, her sensuous fingertips meeting around the rim of the cup.

I lowered my voice. 'What did you mean, yesterday, when you said you were a jailbird?'

'I was found guilty of a breach of the peace after breaking into Oakington detention centre and was jailed for seven days when I refused to be bound over. Not very exciting.'

'It didn't change your mind about being so active?'

'Luckily the people at the Mitchell are only concerned that I put in a 38-hour week: a friend of mine who wasn't arrested phoned them for a week's leave of absence, which I took in lieu of holiday. No questions asked. Directly. But then of course ...'

'But then ...', I interposed after her intentional pause, 'I take it that your involvement with the forces of law and order will be on your personnel records at the Mitchell just as they will be on every other security computer.'

'You're quick on the uptake,' she said with friendly irony. 'Oh, the implication's clear enough. I toe the line from now on or there won't be any place for me in Glasgow District Libraries. After all, can they hold my job open for a jailbird?'

'You couldn't sue them for unjustifiable dismissal?'

'I could, but they'd think of another reason for dismissing me.'

'And are there others?'

'Could be.'

'Tell me.'

'Let's get outside, Davie.'

I paid for the coffees, and we linked arms as we sped downhill like a couple of teenagers in love. 'What does your husband do, Julia?' She smiled, and ran ahead of me, making for Sauchiehall Street, and the second of our rendezvous at my hotel. I asked for my key. A black-haired girl of about 22 was standing by the reception desk. She extended her beautifully-manicured right hand towards me. 'Hello,' she said. 'I'm Tamara.' I looked round in alarm, but Julia was nowhere to be seen. 'It's alright,' said the girl. 'Julia said she'd leave us alone this morning.' She seemed to have the trace of an Eastern European accent, and a fragrance coming from her white polo-necked sweater as well as from her attractive face, with delicate features and a small nose, bell-like earrings dangling from her pretty ears. I recollected something that Julia had said the day before: 'plenty of girls in Glasgow', 'little Tamara Ransome', 'I've told her all about you.' I felt a drought in my throat from nervous excitement.

'Julia said you were interested in Ansari.'

She stood against the door, once I had locked it again from the inside. 'O Lord, I, a beggar,' she recited, 'ask of Thee, More than a thousand kings may ask of Thee; Each one has something he needs to ask of Thee. I have come to ask Thee to give me Thyself.'

Her tiny, neat crimson fingernails drew two lines from my chin back to the lobes of my ears and she pulled my head down to her lips. I forced my hands behind her body, down the door's

wood, to feel the mounds of her small buttocks as they writhed and parted. I felt her skirt drop gently on to my feet.

When I pulled her to the bed, she said 'I used to be greatly troubled with greasy skin.' I found a sheath in my sponge-bag, and fitted it on, as she gazed up at my erection. 'Urged by desire,' I murmured to the alert girl, as she breathed hard, 'I wandered in the streets of good and evil. I gained nothing but intensifying fires of desire.' I kissed the black hair that she had spread out like Medusan snakes, then her cheeks, her lips, her nipples, and the white skin above her panties. She would not remove her panties at all, but wrestled with my hands, making me yelp as she scratched.

She whispered: 'Know, friend, human sorrow springs from three things: To want before it is due, To want more than the allotted share, To want for oneself what belongs to others.' I was tormented with desire for her body, which I had never even seen a few minutes before. 'To want before it is due'. I caressed her shoulders, sucked her earlobes, and ran my hands down her sides and across her soft white belly. She had closed her eyes, and her delicate hands were poised in the air, tensely splayed. 'Shahrazad', I breathed inaudibly. In real life we should have consummated this extraordinary meeting of two perfect strangers, but she was a creature of fantasy, like myself, able to enter the crevices of imagination and remain there without the faintest echo of the rough voice of reality. We stayed within our own web: she a squirming, long-legged victim, trapped and defenceless, I a marauding carnivore, relentless in the touch of hands and mouth. At one point she allowed her tongue to lick vividly at my bare shoulder; at another her fingernails crept up my legs to prick my scrotum. But her dark-stained panties were not pulled down. I lay along her length, then turned over on back and pulled her above me, feeling my cock hard against the silk of her panties, but she did not kiss me, her eyes closed.

🐝 22 🐝

Then there was a knock on the door. I rolled off the bed and went to the door, while Tamara sat on the bed, facing the window opposite the door.

'Who is it?'

'Julia.' Pause. Then Tamara: 'It's alright: let her in.'

I foolishly put on my shirt and trousers. I unlocked the door, and Julia came in. I suddenly remembered: 'To want for oneself what belongs to others', but there was no guilt in the mutual gaze of Julia and Tamara. There was constraint, perhaps. A vague hint of conspiracy? Of course, for Julia had introduced us. Why?

Julia came over to kiss me, perfunctorily, and with no recognition of my sexual desire. 'Can you leave us alone, together, Davie?'

'Of course,' I said, chivalrously, but what could have persuaded me to let the vibrant Julia remain in a bedroom alone with the near-naked Tamara? As I straightened my tie, and squirted hot water into a paper cup with chicken-soup powder, I thought of going back into my room, where I had just seen Tamara lie back on my bed. But my unfulfilled assignation with Julia yesterday and the resolutely incomplete entanglement with Tamara led me to one inescapable conclusion: that I was being used as a decoy by two women. Each had aroused herself with me, and sated herself with the other. Is this why Julia had spent so many weekends at demonstrations with other women, as men spend weekends with their rugby clubs?

I waited outside my room, on a chair as if in a maternity hospital waiting-room, awaiting the nurse's verdict. 'It's a girl,' I whispered, 'it's a girl.' It was too early for lunch, and in any case I could hardly go out in this cold Glasgow morning without jacket or coat, which were left in my wardrobe.

After fifteen minutes or so, the door opened softly and Tamara emerged, flushed, fully-dressed, smiling at me as if in secret confirmation of a famous victory. I knocked, and re-entered. Julia was applying lipstick with an air of concentration that a cat employs when washing its belly.

'Well?' I said, in a tone between severity and mock-severity, so that either interpretation might catch her out. 'Well?' she echoed. Then eventually, she added, 'Did you find Tamara pleasing?'

'I might well have,' I replied, 'if Tamara had been left to her own devices. As it is, I am wearing a sheath that I have not had the chance to use, and I should like to use it now.'

She waited until I approached, then unzipped my trousers, removed the sheath, and began to stroke and rub my cock until it achieved its former size and length. Then she pulled it too hard and made it feel sore, without coming to ejaculation. 'Finish it yourself, Davie,' she said, tonelessly.

'Have you no interest in men, any more?'

'Interest is a funny word, Davie. I find them interesting enough, but as objects of curiosity more than affection or love.' Stately, blue-eyed, she could have become a great administrator or politician with her persuasive voice and magnetic personality. But she had become disenchanted with the mechanics of political power and the way that divisions are manufactured. I relieved myself into the washbasin and flushed away the passion that Julia and Tamara had engendered but left unfulfilled.

'Women have the past, present, and future of the world at the tips of their fingers,' she said, and I noted that her mood was no longer flippant, as it had been the day before. 'The ability to arouse men is a small enough accomplishment, but it will serve until we have control of something more than that. You know the police at Rosyth and Lakenheath hate us because so many of us were openly affectionate with each other? Why do you think it is so distasteful to caress each other, when we are not adding to the evils of overpopulation and starvation? Why did the police call us "lezzies" as a term of abuse? Och, you'll never understand it because you think of women as a kind of inferior race who minister to the wants of their erring menfolk. One side: hefty, strong, thinking, inventive, creative men. The other: pusillanimous, weak, mindless, repetitive, gormless women.'

'I didn't say any of that, Julia. If you knew me, you'd know that I love and respect and admire many women – more women than men.'

'It's the assumptions of the British ruling classes, and you know it. When you took me to Aldeburgh, you were telling me in so many words that I was the little woman being judged for suitability in bed, for manners, accent, dress, make-up, posture, horsy or doggy subjects. You were supposed to be judged on your masculinity, generosity, sense of humour, kindness. We both had to be "nice" to each other, and damn the rest of the starving, miserable ancient world crumbling, festering and dying beyond the safety of the North Sea, and the comfortable cushion of those dependable Vikings in Scandinavia, or those reliable Germans who could soak up the bad news of Rwanda or Cambodia before it could reach our eyes and ears. Did you ever see David Attenborough smiling out from this television pictures of "The Living Planet" and wonder why there were no lepers or kids with rickets? Well, I'll tell you. It's because men run the world, pollute the world, misrule the world, and watch it – with some belated misgivings, being destroyed. I'm telling you all this because you're an idle devil and I don't trust you to do anything logical or sensible, but I think you're intelligent enough in a matter of self-interest like the survival of mankind as we know it to put aside your tinkerings with Arabic literature and set your mind to what matters. If you die without achieving anything, well, at least you'll have tried. But some subversives are needed in the world of men, and you're a product of the spy school at Shemlan. If they didn't train you to spy, as well as to speak and read Arabic, at least you'll know where to go if you want to subvert the male chauvinist lobby that stores nuclear missiles in Britain and sells out to the U.S.A.'

'Have you tried joining the Scottish Parliament, Julia?'

She placed her arms akimbo on her knees and snorted. 'All these little groupings are obsolete,' she replied decisively, 'like Esperanto or arming the Falklands'.

'It's kind of you to place so much emphasis on my being able to help.' (Would she resist it if I tried to touch her breasts?)

'I thought it would be no use.'

'Julia, Einstein said that the most incomprehensible thing about the world is that it is comprehensible, and perhaps you seek to make it even more comprehensible by offering large solutions to complex subjects. Your attitudes are what govern your behaviour. You don't seem to think about anything, but only attitudinise. You don't ask what alternative there may be to a pro-American nuclear missile strike force; you only think in one-dimensional terms that you don't like what you see, so you want to pull it down.'

'Of course there are two sides to every question, you idiot, but I'm telling you that we have only been allowed to see one side up until now: the masculine side, with its platonic ideal forms to which no real forms ever actually apply. Utopia should be spelt Utopius, because it is an exclusively male notion. Women get used to making the best of a bad job, while men can only dream about what might be perfect, but is in fact quite unattainable.'

'Whatever did you learn at Cambridge, Julia, if you didn't learn how to dream and *then* try to put those dreams into practice?'

'I learnt that Arabic is a language of great formal beauty wrecked by the laziness and clumsiness and ignorance of the people who speak it.'

'But then you turned to English for some kind of help in making the best of a bad job.'

She looked at me sharply, as though I were trying to condescend. But my face was half turned away, towards the windows set at intervals in the huge back wall of the tenement building opposite.

'I turned to English for a kind of clarity in my means of expressing myself and understanding others.'

'A room of your own.'

'Rolfsson showed me that English may have its own advantages over Cheremis or Sogdian, but it has even more disadvantages. When an Englishman says "You throw it", he feels that he has said something clear and definite. But a Navaho would require the sentence to state whether the "you" is singular or plural; whether "it" is a general or specific object; whether "it" is short, square, dead, liquid, and so on, changing the verb-stem accordingly; whether the act of throwing is about to begin, about to end, in progress once, or in progress habitually; and whether the agent is more or less in control of the throw.'

'You might have been better advised to switch from Arabic to symbolic logic or maths. English is bogged down by its historical impedimenta. When we say e^2 we just mean e^2, but when we say "impedimenta" we also mean strictly "baggage" and less strictly "an army's travelling equipment" as well as "whatever hinders progress".'

'As recently as Heraclitus, nouns we think of as abstract, like "progress" or "willingness", were still considered as concrete as "box" or "mountain", so that human beings, when they spoke of an agreement or a war, thought first of a physical object called "agreement" which corresponded in shape and size and texture to whatever was agreed, and an object called "war", sometimes personified (Mars, Ares) and sometimes thingified (polemos, bellum) but never a purely mental construct.'

'You think that when men began to abandon the physical sense of reality corresponding to their thoughts, they began to lose touch with reality altogether?'

'Well, don't you?'

'Possibly. But I can't help thinking that our thinking has advanced beyond the old Greek concreteness. We don't believe with Thales any more that everything is made up of water.'

'David Quitregard, I have spent enough years in huge libraries to know that 99.9% of all books are senseless maunderings around meaningless propositions endlessly repeated. I used to read Tolstoy because he seemed to be arriving from *The Cossacks* and *War and Peace* by way of the meretricious *Anna Karenina* towards *Resurrection* and an anti-literary summation of life. But he over-romanticised the peasant, and he made his wife's life hell on earth and his children's an unendurable misery.'

'Do you remember what he said about the little green stick?'

'What little green stick?'

'How his elder brother had buried, somewhere in the forest near Yasnaya Polyana, a little green stick carved with a secret formula which, once dug up and spread by word of mouth, would inaugurate a new golden age of universal brotherly love.'

'Utopius', snapped Julia, becoming for an instant herself at the age of sixty. I reduced her tension by massaging her neck and shoulders, so that she relaxed, but she fended my hands away from her breasts.

'Julia, shall we bury a little green stick in the grounds above Kelvin Way?'

'What would *you* write on it?'

'My secret formula? Every woman shall be satisfied. If there are too many women to be paired with men, then let men have more than one woman, or let women live together in peace and harmony.'

She relaxed further, tolerating my mischievous suggestions as appropriate to a bedroom where she had just made love to Tamara and – in a more half-hearted way last night – to me.'

'Tell me about Tamara.'

'Her father was a Scot from Greenock who had an engineering contract in Tblisi, and married a Georgian Jewess. Tamara is the second child; the eldest, a boy, was picked up by the KGB for alleged anti-state activities, which could have meant anything from smuggling jeans to wanting to emigrate to Israel.'

'How did Tamara get out?'

'Her father came out with Tamara, and left the wife and the boy there, both trying to get an exit visa for Israel.'

I continued to stroke her thighs, but with growing frustration. It was lunch-time; I was very hungry; and I was about to enjoy no more illicit love with this blue-eyed iceberg who had just enjoyed Tamara.

I was suddenly fed up with Julia, her intolerance of intolerance, and her insistence on a better world through direct action. For all her incessant propaganda, what had she achieved? Does it not make her tired that even *Lysistrata* was written by a man? That there has been a rapid increase in the battering of women since the expansion of women's refuges? That women, too, snore? That old women grow moustaches, beards, and hair on their arms and legs?

One last throw: I tried Herrick.

'Some ask'd me where the rubies grew,
And nothing did I say,
But with finger pointed to
The lips of Julia.'

'Do you want to know about my diamond ring?' she responded.

'Of course.'

'Her name is Maureen Colquhoun. We have been living together for two years. She is forty-six, and I have never been unfaithful to her before today. I used your room for an assignation with Tamara. We fell in love at the Mitchell Library, but I never dared to ask her before yesterday.'

'You used my name as well.'

'It was a pretext for her father, and for her friends. Women's love is still a crime in Russia and it is frowned upon in Calvinist Scotland to the point where I believe her father might kill her if he finds out.'

'Her father thinks she has been meeting me?'

'At the Seminar. She is studying Arabic and Persian.'

'I know. She quoted me Ansari: "Human sorrow springs from the desire to want for oneself what belongs to others."'

'And you think I belong to Maureen Colquhoun.'

'You do, apparently, otherwise you would not wear her ring.' I withdrew my cock from my trousers again, and ran Julia's ring-finger along its length, so that the ring's sharpness made me yelp, slightly delayed, as if from an electric shock. Erect again. She stroked it more gently, as if in a gesture of farewell or reconciliation: I knew it was farewell.

'Kiss it, Julia.' She shook her head, but for some reason I kissed her wavy hair in affection. She put me back, and zipped up my trousers again.

'Give me lunch, Davie. I know a good Chinese restaurant. You're due back at the Seminar at two.'

At the Golden Dragon, fencing and feinting, Julia and I played out the last of our dialogues. Between us stood a communal bowl of steamed rice, spare ribs, pancake rolls, sweet and sour pork, egg foo yung and king prawns. At Aldeburgh we had begun to explore our differences, minimising them for the sake of pre-marital felicity. Had she even then preferred the bodies of women to mine? Had she held back? I scarcely remembered, for I was buried in my own adventure. I was surprised, I recall, by the way she had showed me how to use a vibrator on all her most sensitive skin inside and out, as well as on my own genitals. She had asked me to use it on her, and seemed to get aroused much more easily than by my hands caressing her breasts and cunt. Or was that only a false memory, distorted by my perception of recent events?

She spoke little. I believe she was thinking about breaking with Maureen for a younger woman. But did she feel as passionately about Tamara as I did? Or as she thought that she did? Had their meeting been an anticlimax today?

What was Julia doing with her life that was so much more urgent or important? She clearly looked down on me; but was it because I fitted her image of the boring male chauvinist, or because I had disappointed her expectations of me as someone who might change the world for what she considered the better?

'Julia, did I disappoint you? What did you expect of me?'

'Nothing. I was flattered that you wanted me, and I made sure that my contemporaries knew I had spent the weekend with you.'

'It gave you a conventional portrait to show off. Were you making love to women then? Or was it that my performance was so unsatisfactory that you turned away from all men in disgust?'

Her smile became ironically admiring – intended to disguise all her feelings under those multiple layers of deception that in Blake too are taken for innocence.

'You think you must be inadequate if I prefer a beautiful Russian girl's body to yours?'

'My inadequacy is a side issue. I am curious to know what you were thinking all those years ago when you seemed to be enamoured of me.'

'Who can ever remember? What does it matter? We didn't talk so much, analyse so much, in those days.'

'I was happy to be with you.'

'Why did you not try to meet me again? Did you have some premonition that our lives could never run parallel, but only cross at odd intervals, by quirks of fortune?'

'I should have been too happy with you. Your demands are made more of yourself than of others. I should have felt strange not providing for a wife, and not being provided for, but living on equal terms. Men are not yet prepared for that decisive shock, when their rule is neither accepted nor rejected, but silently replaced by the sly energy of the New Woman, who has married him, borne him children, and then taken her place again in the world outside, where the stakes are even, for the first time, and the prizes even too.'

'You always said that women were too people-conscious to become like James Joyce, Wagner, or Paul Klee. Their sense of proportion does not allow them that obsessive monomania which enables a genius to burgeon and change our

115

perceptions. Can you imagine Dalí without Gala? Oh yes. Oh no. That is irrelevant. But Gala without Dalí has no sense. That, I remember well, was your final, telling denunciation of women. As if it was of any significance to you, me, or the argument. Or perhaps it was significant to you. You, a man under siege, felt stronger as if Dalí's strength was somehow also your strength. I never bothered to underline the illogicality of all that.'

'But you did say that an awareness of Gala's inherence in Dalí's work made sense of it. That Dalí, and, oh, Picasso, and Leonardo, and all the rest, were like infants trying to understand with their mind and their hands, doodling and jotting, what their mothers already knew and took for granted. The history of painting – and I blushed like any man at the thought of it – was a kind of mad rush of men sketching

116

animals on prehistoric walls or nudes on canvas to find out what it was their wives, and mothers, and sisters, and lovers were trying to tell them by stretching out their hands towards them as in the Uffizi Madonna Doni of Michelangelo, or the London Virgin of the Rocks of Leonardo, or the Giovanna Cenami by Jan van Eyck.'

I stopped for breath, conscious that I was being made ridiculous by a kind of justification for what I could not believe in. This was a picture of the history of creation – that is, in my reading of it, of man's creation – which had been invented or recreated by Julia as a reductio ad absurdum to show the strangeness of all art history. You always stood outside the paintings, looking in, and linking together masterpieces in the Boijmans-van Beuningen Museum, or the Budapest Museum, cross-referencing, comparing and making your own imaginary museum which consisted of all the great paintings in the world. You never thought that those who knew only the East German galleries could not be familiar, simply by museumgoing, with the Australian galleries. Just as you never really comprehended how those who could only read Arabic would never realise that 'literature' meant to those who could only read Polish. You always assumed some kind of consensus, some nebulous Unesco-like conference hall where Senegalese speaking French with cultured Argentinians would somehow be talking about the *same things* because they were using the same words, and cordially agreeing with each other.

No: the links were always false. Tamara could speak Georgian, Russian, English, Persian, Arabic, but she would be infinitely different from her Georgian mother, her British father, the Russian authorities, the Glasgow taxi-drivers, the poets who intoned Persian, the linguists who expounded Arabic to her and listened to her broken plurals in a Russian accent.

117

And Julia herself? She too had no connection with me or with Tamara that could not be rudely and abruptly shattered by transposition to Washington or Moscow, by a sex weekend in Aldeburgh eight years ago, or stray meetings in a Glasgow bedroom yesterday and today.

Julia was eating sedately and slowly, as if she were being watched by examiners for good breeding. Even now, after we had somehow sealed our acquaintanceship with an auld lang syne, she remained aloof, treating me as if I had been an animal let out from the zoo for one meal but had to be guarded carefully in case I made a false move – a getaway over the rooftops. I savoured our last moments together, exactly as Shahrazad had relished the first minutes, each night, when it was revealed that she had at least that coming night and coming day to live. Like me, she had to weave another story that would be entertaining to those around her. I had to justify my existence by working for Sophie, chairing a ferocious seminar meeting on the Palestinian poets, or preparing for my next class.

I paid the bill; Julia reimbursed half by slipping ten pounds into my pocket. 'Not a word' and after a quick kiss on the cheek she strode away down Sauchiehall Street. I felt dismissed. For a moment I could not visualise Blanche Afanasian: I saw only Julia, sitting in the chair in my bedroom, smiling tolerantly at my lustful body: that absurd male body, without the all-saving, celebratory womb. She had made her point. Too many points. I felt she owned Glasgow, like a mafiosa City Mother, a Mayoress, a princess allowed for a few minutes the ineffable gift of private ecstasy with another woman, out of the public glare. Victor Napcott would have classed her among the masters, at that moment, and me among the slaves.

❦ 23 ❧

To show my face as an alibi: yes, I was there and nowhere else. That was my motive in returning to the lecture theatre. In the back row Shaikha Haya and Zaid looked somnolent but watchful, like a pair of cats. In front of them, at the sparsely-attended early afternoon lecture on developments in Tunisian prose given by Carl Harbick, sat the hunched figure of Vanderpoel, the sardonic Olithorn making notes, an East European I knew only as Jerzy, a Pakistani girl from Birmingham, and a dozen others.

Sam Glotz bustled in as quietly as his barrel-bulk would permit, and patted me on the back. I moved discreetly to the front row, so that everyone could see me, and made notes, apparently on Harbick's lecture but in fact on the rest of the afternoon. I could pick up a girl off the streets, or stay here with the maunderings of Harbick dulling my senses with their nasal drone. I could see the house of Charles Rennie Mackintosh. No, what was I thinking of? It had to be the Burrell.

Fitzstephen Leggate pushed open the door with a flourish at once military and pedantic, and closed it with a careful click, pushing it up boldly then at the precise instant when it would otherwise have slammed he pulled up short like James

Dean on the chicken run. I felt in my pocket for my mobile phone to call Cambridge. First Corinne at the Faculty. I made way, half-smiling, half-nodding at the deeply-lined face of Leggate, who had spent formative years with King Abdulaziz in Saudi Arabia, and forever regaled those around him with diplomatic and financial anecdotes which may even have been genuine. He brushed past me with a forbidding stare reserved for those younger than himself, a class comprising most of the world's population. I phoned Sophie first.

'Hello, David here. How are things? Deadly. Duty makes us all a little ridiculous, doesn't it? Neil and Jamila send their best. It'll probably go on for three or four days more. Then there's the next Seminar to fix up. Expect me when I turn up. Andy and Neil keeping you busy?'

I phoned Corinne second, but there was no urgent business for me at the Faculty: Yukič was seeing to that, and delegating my work to Shambles and Runson.

Thirdly I phoned directory enquiries for the Newport Post Office, and enquired whether they had on their notice-board a card for 'Tithe Barn Antiques', carefully disguising my voice as a mournful Glaswegian with laryngitis. No.

I phoned the Tithe Barn in the hope of hearing Rose's voice, but heard Napcott's yap on the answerphone.

I leapt into a passing taxi: 'The Burrell Collection', and twenty minutes later, through a number of strange, unlikely Glasgows, I arrived in Pollok Park, its woods and meadows culminating in a stark, church-like wooden door. The driver stopped, and I got out and paid with a ten-pound note. I had only an hour and a half before the museum closed, so I decided to concentrate on the Chinese ceramics, a resolution overthrown at once by the magical profusion of tapestries from the fifteenth and sixteenth centuries. Radiant among them was 'The Pursuit of Fidelity', from Alsace, showing two lovers on horseback pursuing a stag into a net: their hunt seemed destined to end in success. The Franco-Netherlandish 'Camel Caravan' is a tapestry very much larger and more ambitious, its serpentine-necked camels causing understandable bewilderment in the streets of sixteenth-century Antwerp.

While rapt in the extraordinary stained glass, such as the or and gules 'Solomon and Queen of Sheba' from Germany, I kept an eye open for lonely women I could accompany out of the building as closing-time drew near. An adventure so far from home could hardly embarrass Sophie or anyone else. Apart from schoolchildren and old ladies peering at the captions in a vain effort to remember names and dates, I saw nobody I could take back to Sauchiehall Street.

Outside the glass walls autumn leaves were being thrashed down by vehement winds; a hint of drizzle made me shiver. A woman in her forties dressed in red, with a crocodile-skin handbag, passed me on her way to the exit. She looked energetic, rather hard, with that calculating makeup that looks imposed by a professional dresser rather than visualised by the woman herself. Mascara, lipstick exactly shaped to the lips' edges, powder levelling incipient ridges on the face and neck. She walked purposefully to a Peugeot in the car park. It was empty. I made the move.

'Excuse me, do you know where the taxi-rank is? I have to get back to Central Glasgow for a Seminar in Arabic Literature.'

'Which part?' She seemed not to be sizing me up, but the trace of an Amazon's smile momentarily relaxed the corners of her attractive mouth.

'Anywhere near the University will do.'

'Get in.'

'I hope it's not taking you out of your way?'

'Have you a cigarette?'

'I'm afraid I don't smoke.'

'You study or teach?'

'I teach.'

She lit her own cigarette, and waited for my next move.

'You enjoyed the Burrell?'

'I always do. Do you know what happens to a harvest mouse when it senses the tiniest vibration, noise, or change in silhouette?'

'No.'

'At first it keeps absolutely still, learning what kind of change has occurred in its brief existence.'

'And then?'

'You can imagine.'

'I should think it scatters as fast as it can, to deceive potential enemies.'

'Only in the case of violent disturbance, like the approach of a threshing machine. In the case of ambiguous menaces, it steals softly away, like a thief in the night, slowly and silently. It can tell the difference between a violent threat and a possible disturbance, and knows how to act accordingly.'

'You know a great deal about harvest mice.'

'It is my job. I'm a government scientist seconded to investigate the spread of the harvest mouse to the Lowlands.'

'You mean the harvest mouse is not indigenous to the Lowlands?' I accompanied this question by putting my right hand on her left knee.

'Until a few years ago there were hardly any harvest mice north of the Borders, but there has been a sudden swing to Ayrshire, and the population is increasing by leaps and bounds.' She rested her left palm lightly on my right hand, with the most sensitive touch. She had still not started the car. I moved my hand below her skirt, more and more boldly, with no resistance. Darkness was approaching, and the car park was emptying rapidly. Soon ours was the only car left, apart from an Audi Avant a hundred yards away.

Her panties were wet; I began to rub the external lips, then probed inside with one finger, and then with two. 'In the wild, female harvest mice attain sexual maturity at about 45 days, but this can be contracted to 35 days in captivity, giving birth seventeen days later.'

She explored my legs, at first gently, then quickly, restlessly, urgently. She lifted her head to be kissed, and we brought each other to some sort of climax very quickly.

'When mating is complete,' she said, after clearing her throat, and wiping her hands on a tissue from her handbag, 'the female often turns on the male, who will never play any further part in building a nest or rearing the young. The nestlings and the female together weigh several times as much as the nest, but its strength and elasticity are so powerful that its inmates are not at risk.' We drove along the A77 towards the city.

'You wouldn't care to come back to my hotel?'

'While suckling one litter, the harvest mouse is usually pregnant with the next, and in captivity will produce a new litter every three or four weeks.'

'I'd like to sleep with you tonight.'

'Though the mother looks after the family single-handed, there is very little morality within litters. Runts are not unknown, but a mother will normally ensure that they survive to weaning.'

'You don't have to go home, do you?'

'Adult males are vociferous when mating, and violent when quarrelling, biting at their enemies' rump, tail and ears.'

I attempted to pull her hand towards me to kiss her again, but she roughly pushed me away to concentrate on driving in the dark rain. Lampposts seemed halfhearted in their attempts to bring us light. Our tyres spat spray on the pavements, so that pedestrians had to skip back nervously or crossly from the kerb.

I asked, 'Do you dream about harvest mice?'

'No: I dream about being killed by huge express trains, one after the other. I can never get out of the way. It's because I'm a Pisces connected with Taurus: the headlong flight to destruction.'

'Gadarene swine?'

'I suppose so.'

'How do you collect harvest mice?'

'In milk bottles placed upright in tall grass below a nest. But you've got to check the bottle very frequently to make sure the mouse doesn't die. It will die, if wet, within half an hour, because it can't keep warm enough.'

'Could you let me off at Sauchiehall Street, the west end, at my hotel? I've something to fetch before I go back to the Seminar.

'You're not going to the Seminar this evening, are you?'

'Not if you'll spend the night with me, with or without harvest mice.'

'I'll put you down at Sauchiehall Street. There are plenty of wee lassies who'll be glad of the custom.'

She pulled up quickly by a darkened doorway; within its shadows two girls were chatting. Office girls? Possibly.

'Take your pick,' said my chauffeuse.

'Thanks for the ride,' I said.

'You're not far from the University,' she said, and drove off.

24

I pulled my raincoat collar up to try to keep some of the rain from saturating my neck, shoulders, back. The two girls made way for me in the doorway between them. One was a negress, with full red lips, a head shorter than myself, with an umbrella that looked as if it might be used threateningly. The other was a pert, ill-cosmeticked blonde in an imitation fur coat flecked with rain drops, and green gloves. Both were chewing gum in a restless manner copied from gangster movies. I thought of the third and fifth of 'Los bens de fortuna' listed in *Tirant lo Blanc*: 'Lo primer és grans riquees. Lo segon grans honors. Lo terç bella muller. Lo quart molts infants. Lo cinquè gràcia de gents.' A fair wife, and grace in company. A fair woman. I wanted the negress, but Martorell persuaded me towards the blonde.

'How much?' I said.

'Ten for a quickie, fifty all nigh'.'

She was fleecing me, trying it on, because I was in my best suit. To avoid losing face with the seductive negress, I agreed, 'Ten, then, come to the hotel up the road.'

I thought about borrowing the umbrella, but one more look at the feline negress and I preferred to propel the blonde along with me. The rain showed every sign of becoming heavier: the deluge I could imagine provoking honest burghers of Glasgow into fashioning arks in the nearest open space.

The blonde pulled herself away from my protective arm; on her high heels she evidently felt insecure if unexpectedly touched.

'You're not from these parts?'

'Come from London. How about you?'

'I'm English too.'

'This where you're staying?'

'Just for a few days.'

I took my room key from the same receptionist who had seen me arrive first with Julia, then with Tamara. I might have come earlier with the harvest-mouse specialist, but instead, such are the antics of men in need of succour, I arrive with a Cockney whore as if I were in the Old Kent Road.

'Got anything to drink, any hash?'

'No. There's chicken soup in the corridor.'

She looked at me as if I were joking at her expense.

She slipped off her fur coat as I closed the door.

'Do you want to know my name?' she says to me, and I says to 'er, 'Only if you don't want to know mine.' She looked at a hastily-scrawled name on the top of a pile of Seminar papers on my table by the wash-basin: 'It's Neil Strutt,' she said in unmistakeable triumph.

She was now naked down to the kind of black bra and panties she must have imagined Marilyn Monroe in. 'Say goodbye to Pat, say goodbye to Jack, and say goodbye to yourself,' I

126

murmured just loudly enough for her to overhear, 'because you're a nice guy.'

I thought of her as 'she' in the third person, never as second-person 'you'; 'you' is bisexual but 'she' remains resolutely woman-sexy. I could see how Julia Baneath could writhe and achieve orgasm at the thought of 'she' next to 'she'. Could she have abandoned Arabic because 'he', 'huwa' and 'she', 'hiya', both had feminine endings, rendering the difference between the straight man and the curved woman insignificant?'

The blonde was fitting a sheath on to me.

'Aren't you on the pill?'

'Course, but I like it better this way.'

'Take it off. I'm paying the tenner. I'll have it the way I like.'

She sulked. 'Take it off yourself.'

I did, but my heat was retreating into petulance. She could not have been more than eighteen, and behaved like a ten-year-old. I longed to dislodge her blonde wig but I allowed her that flattery. She aroused me by stroking her breasts, and rubbing the nipples between thumb and index finger, eyes closed. She moved her right hand down between her legs, continuing to excite me, if not herself, by a manoeuvre she must often have repeated. Her fingers were too short, but made up for that deficiency by agility. She was keener to please than she would have owned. And it was clear that she traded her body not only for easy money, but also because she derived at least some temporary satisfaction from seeing how skilfully she could help men release their tensions. As I lay on my back, with my legs stretched out, she sat on my erect prick and stretched herself over me, drawing up her knees to her stomach. Then she rested her hands on my shoulders and pulled herself up, nuzzling my lips, first closed, then open, then tantalisingly closed.

She quickly brought me to ejaculation, and seemed to reach some kind of enjoyment herself, but that may have been pure pretence. 'Sure you don't want to spend the other forty?'

'I'd love to,' replied the bogus Strutt, 'but I can't afford it.'

'Neither can I', she retorted, matter-of-fact.

'Thanks anyway,' I said, as she was dressing quickly. I found her a ten-pound note in my wallet, and handed it to her with a slight bow, which she pretended not to notice. 'You're welcome to stay till the rain stops.'

'In *Glasgow?*' she answered incredulously, feeling to see if her fur coat had dried in the warm room.

'See ya,' she said, clicking her high heels in the harlot's equivalent of a goose-step. I wondered when she would give up the life: probably after a knife had shortened her career. A knife in the neck, shoulder, arm, ankle, heart: your whole future is determined by which part of the anatomy the knife penetrates, and how far.

25

At one point I had asked Sophie if she would let me graze her skin with a dagger, or let a penknife-point touch the taut skin of her breast without drawing blood but just leaving a faint red pin-prick, detectable only by the connoisseur, only for a few moments. By the deductive and inductive powers of a Sherlock Holmes of sexual passion. Homer somewhere notes to his own evident surprise the 'relishing of pain' which culminates in the Marquis de Sade and our modern concentration camps. No sexual passion by pain after Auschwitz? Sophie agreed until she saw the rusty dagger, and the neat boy-scout penknife. Then she refused, as if the concept were agreeable, but the moment unpropitious, or the sight of metal atavistically terrible. I offered no threat: only pleasure. But she eventually refused, and that night we did not make love.

The only woman I had tortured was Margot Liddell, a nurse at Addenbrooke's who had been one of those looking after me while I was undergoing a minor skin operation.

I had invited Margot back to my lodgings, and she had made the kind of hungry love by which some nurses try to rid themselves of the spectres of disease and death: a kind of fantasy-oblivion between the pink foamy Land of Cartland and the glitzy, tough and glamorous State of California. She wanted to marry a surgeon or, if not, a doctor, but until then an affair with a young man back from the Middle East would do. She did not naturally scrub all the natural oils out of her skin at nights and weekends, but only before reporting back for shift-work, where you would not have distinguished her from any other brisk girl in uniform.

We were both twenty-two, six years ago. I showed her the Islamic departments of the Victoria and Albert Museum, and Leighton House. She didn't ask me to become a Catholic, like herself, because she imagined I was a Muslim, a mistake I never troubled to contradict. If she had thought I was a religious sceptic, I somehow concluded, she would urge me to convert. She always told me her dreams, primly folding her arms like a mixed infant at Sunday school as she unfolded a reel of horrors, such as being trampled on by a herd of rogue elephants with blood billowing out of their mouths, tusks elongated to fearsome dimensions. Or she would be drowning, clasped to the oceanbed by the longing tentacles of a remorseless octopus. She saw the entire natural world as a kind of Roman Colosseum, and herself the sole defenceless prisoner being assaulted by armed gladiators or ravenous lions.

I pointed out that being tied up and whipped was a pleasure sought by many women; it did not take long before she shyly asked what I wanted to do with her, and I pretended that I didn't want anything to do with her and would only do it if she pleaded with me on bended knee. This she immediately did, with tears of pleasure or terror in her eyes. I kicked her gently, then harder until I bruised both arms and both legs. Later on I found a heavy rope and tied her tightly to a kitchen chair in my room. She would let me punish only the parts of her body normally covered by nurse's uniform, so the gag over her mouth had to be loose.

I used to pull her black hair until she screamed, so the gag was a necessary precaution. Once the landlady, Mrs Bogallan, complained about hearing a shriek, but I explained that I had seen a boy chasing a cat with a brick, and this explanation seemed to satisfy her. Then, since Margot worked shifts, it was often possible for her to come round while Mrs Bogallan was out shopping or visiting her aunt in St Eligius St.

Then I would undress Margot, tie her with ropes and a chain chafing her genitals to a chair, and beat her breasts with a rope until they became raw and red, with drops of blood hanging from her nipples like dripping grape juice from the muslin my mother had filled to make grape jelly in my childhood. I pulled the heavy chain around her buttocks until she jerked convulsively with the sudden pain. I slapped her face gently with my palm open, then savagely bit her thighs.

Our lovemaking afterwards was flurried and only partly ecstatic, for Margot would often wince whenever I touched her bruised flesh. But she would always return to me, over a period of five to six weeks, until she suddenly disappeared from Addenbrooke's, and the personnel department gave me no forwarding address. She had clearly moved right away. I had only one photograph to remind me of her: it showed her long nose, but her heavy, wary eyes were half-shut, and you could not even make out that they were black, like her hair. She was tall, but a slightly stooping gait made her seem of medium height. Her voice was soft in speech, but occasionally raucous in laughter. Her family was Scottish, but had lived in southern England so long that they had lost their accent, and Margot had even affected a few mannerisms of the English, like 'Gawd!' or 'Strewth!' She put up her hands to her mouth when laughing, as if stifling a belch, but she clearly saw laughter as a duty rather than a pleasure, and her sense of humour was limited and unpredictable.

What drew me to Margot was her desire for suffering at my hands. She was generous with money, too, and once gave me her whole week's wage when I took her away for a weekend at Frinton. The weekend was entirely wasted, because she developed a bad cold, and spent both days and nights shivering and sneezing. I went to Clacton for fish and chips, which is all she wanted to eat. And Tolly Cobbold beer, I remember.

I had no desire to make Margot suffer without her full, even delirious consent. She would read *Woman's Weekly* stories while sitting on the toilet, rapt in the autumn sunshine of the Manor Farm where Ralph and Dolores gazed arm in arm over the rolling acres, he with brylcreemed hair and she with mischievous dimples, both revealing even teeth brushed dazzling white every forty-five minutes. Then she would stretch full-length on a sheepskin rug while I roped her wrists to the bed-post and pulled a twenty-pronged garden rake down from her shoulder to her ankles, slapping her whenever she cried in pain. At first she made love frantically, passionately, after these incidents, calling me 'Tom' – I later found out she thought of me in her fantasy as Tom Cruise, but the confusion was real enough when it happened. Then she became less interested in me as a man, and more as an inflictor of torment: a one-man Chamber of Horrors, a Mengele with a human face, a co-operative Mr Hyde. She was not interested in my body, only in hers, and in the violence which it could suffer without swooning. Once I thought she had fainted, but she explained that it was a trance of ecstasy which she compared to the stigmata of a saint. There was no torture she would not undergo for my sake, were her words, but I knew better. The humiliation was entirely for her own sake, and in the end she regarded me as a nameless figment of her long-sought nightmares, indulged and recalled like any faded family photograph.

I never considered her depraved or insane: I understood the logic of her keen sensations, as one will if confronted with

Genet, Fassbinder, Pasolini and their blind crashes into violence. Why should boredom be more proper or more sane than the fiercest excitement? After all, title fights are licit, as are aerobatic displays or solo jungle-faring. Margot Liddell traded her starched nurse's uniform for the evanescent thrills of contacts between her naked body and steel, rope, leather whips, chains, nets drawn tightly around her thighs, cucumbers and bananas thrust deep into her genitals and arse, her mouth gagged and eyes closed as if watching the back of a mirror. Then she would take a bath, heal herself expertly, clinically bring me to my own delayed climax with her tongue and lips, and repossess her nurse's spotless identity with the artless confidence of the world's youngest trickster, who knows that below a certain age even the darkest criminal cannot be correctly punished.

I wanted to find Margot again, because Sophie bore no dark side; she lacked the wounded tigress dimension as she lacked the innocent Judy Garland aspect at the other end of the rainbow. She had been programmed by the Summerburns of Hunstanton and her friends – even her classmates – to fit a placid image of a young mother who would grow middle-aged gracefully, then old with equal staid comfort. I could not imagine Margot middle-aged or old: where could she be?

I knew that Addenbrooke's had no record of her, because I had tried them before, but could there be any friends of hers still nursing there?

26

The next morning was so slow in coming that it was nine-thirty before I realised that night had lost its grip for a few restless hours.

'Quitters,' nattered the unexpected telephone caller, 'is that you?'

'Batty?'

'Sophie gave me your hotel number. Have I interrupted anything?

'Of course not. What do you want?'

'Almost nothing. A mere suggestion.'

'What are you up to?'

'Simply that you can swear on oath that we sat up all night playing pontoon or cribbage or something. In your hotel room. What's the number?'

'254. Look, if I have to testify, don't I hear what I'm testifying about?'

'It's Lizzie, you inmate.'

'What's Lizzie?'

'She's got some silly idea I've been seeing that lodger we had, you know, Blanche whatsername.'

'Afanasian, she's in my group. Well, have you, Batty?'

underground
www.jesusmayball.com

'Nothing of the sort, you inmate.'

'How did Lizzie get the idea?'

'She saw me.'

'Saw you doing what?'

'Mending the strap on her bra, after it broke, and her tits got loose. Could happen to anyone. Perils of having any lodger. If it's a man, the wife gets accused of wanting anything in trousers. If it's a girl, the husband gets accused of wanting anything with a slit skirt.'

'And she is quite attractive.'

'Oh, absolutely. So after Lizzle started bawling me out I drove this Blanche woman out of harm's way.'

'And then you spent the night here with me.'

'In a word, yes.'

'The Inter-City via Edinburgh must have made pretty good time. When did you set out?'

'Oh, I see what you mean. You mean, I only arrived in Glasgow this morning?'

'You probably took the connection at Peterborough via Doncaster and Newcastle, and changed at Edinburgh.'

'And I suppose I got into Glasgow this morning?'

'That's right. Where are you, Batty?'

'Somewhere in the New Forest.'

'With Blanche?'

'No. She wanted to go to some Armenian friends of hers in Coleridge Road, laser people, to stay overnight. I've come down to my sister Pam's while Lizzie cools off. Did you see my bit about the Americas Cup?'

'What bit?'

'It seems all the rags yesterday picked up some tomfool story about a rich Finn making twenty million dollars available for a fellow in the New Forest so that he can make a new yacht from druid oaks in the ancient woodlands to win the Americas Cup.'

'Don't tell me: you're the fellow in the New Forest.'

'And the rich Finn, you inmate. It seems no English reporter can tell the difference over the phone between my Finnish accent and your genuine article.'

'Can you leave me out of the Americas Cup, Batty, if I swear you were playing cribbage here from six o'clock this morning till Lizzie phones? Hey, and what if she wants to speak to you?'

'Oh, cripes, you inmate! You've known me all these years and you still can't manage my accent?'

'Listen, Batty, do you know a nurse called Margot Liddell?'

'No, should I? Has she been complaining?'

'If I have to spend the rest of the morning playing cribbage with you in Glasgow, the least you can do is to establish among your many and varied associates the whereabouts of one Margot Liddell, hair black, eyes black, five feet nine, formerly a nurse at Addenbrooke's Hospital, current whereabouts unknown.'

'Tried the old and trusted?'

'What?'

'Nurses' Register, you inmate. Facts and figures. Is she R.C.N.?'

'I imagine so.'

'Bob's your uncle.' He rang off.

I called the Mitchell, expecting the sultry voice of Julia. But no: it was an adenoidal youth, one of those simple souls who believe that by working in libraries they will acquire by osmosis the genius in every book they touch. They could become the greatest of all authors now, but prefer to defer the hard work till after their immortality.

'Bay I helb you?'

'Could you check the Register of Nurses for Margot Liddell, please?'

'Bargo?'

'Liddell, Bargo Liddell.'

'Hold od a bobud, bleed.'

While the yug bad was bakig edquirid, I ibagid hib bakig up dirtery ribe, like 'Bary, Bary' or 'Liddell Bit Buppet', but gave up with 'Tob, Tob, the Biber's Sud.'

The neglected genius of Mitchell's Reference Library eventually returned. Batty McMan's brainwave had in fact turned up one Bargo Liddell and one Bargaret Liddell. I assured him that he could elibidate Bargaret frob hid idvetigatiod.

'Sevedteed, Royal Cresced, Bath.' I fairly whistled. She hadn't changed her married state, apparently, but she had landed at one of the most intriguing and exhilarating addresses in Europe. Royal Crescent: I felt like exploring Pevsner on Bath before I explored Margot's body again. Would she have a man already resident? Children? Was she a governess or nursemaid to an extraordinary family on the Beau Nash model?

The electoral roll for Bath would supply the answer. I rang Directory Enquiries, then the Reference Library in Bath. Names at 17 Royal Crescent? Afraid we can't give them over the phone, she froze. Could you come in, please? Nod ibediately, Bidid, I'b id Gladgow.

Sophie was not expecting me for several days, and Batty would hardly give the game away, even though he must have realised what game I was chasing. Had he really left Blanche in Cambridge, or was he disrobing her under the grave millennial oaks of the Forest miscalled New? I saw him as a randy Robin Hood pursuing not Maid Marian, oh no, but Shahrazad the enigmatic, the copper-haired. I saw again my vision from the Crusades against Islam: a wimpled countess gazing from her battlements down to a knight in armour whose horse is trampling all over her favourite daffodils.

I packed as quickly as usual, stuffing my nightgear into my case, ran downstairs whistling, like a daredevil lad on the vicar's porch before the solemn face appears, and paid my bill. Then into a taxi, on to the train bound for Bath, change at Birmingham and Bristol.

Across the aisle, all four separate men yakked half of four unimaginably tedious dialogues into four separate mobile phones, gazing into midair or out of the window to avoid catching eyes that questioned them or criticised them for contaminating the original quietness before the train was boarded. I turned for relief to the other maniac at my side, watching him in silent admiration as he tapped his laptop and peered at the shimmering, crackling screen.

'What are you doing?', my courage finally aroused by irritated curiosity.

'This mate? It's a greyhound racing game.'

Mute amazement. 'There are no greyhounds on the train.'

'See, righ?, every few minutes they put this race on. You bet on 1, 2, 3, 4, 5, or 6 – whatever dog you fancy – any number, righ? You wager a quid every time, righ? If it wins, you ge' a fiver.'

'How?'

'Dunno, I never acksherly won anything yet. But, righ, I do know that if you get first and second in the right order, they give you 21 quid.'

'Who do?'

'Search me.'

27

At Bristol I picked a No Smoking compartment, still almost empty twenty minutes before departure.

A railway carriage on the move is a laboratory of human emotions, where we experimental rats sniff and snort, sit or prowl, and ponder various possibilities in the immediate future. How Shahrazad would have charmed the Sultan if she had regaled him with tales of sitting-rooms rushing through fields and cities! How she would have fabricated past, present and future for the sedentary dullards who think Aladdin's lamp is imaginary, and genies a host of inexistences! She did not weave her net of tales to lure the Sultan's attention, but merely used him as a listener to test the plausibility of what she described. It was as true to her as the sea is to bedu in the desert: a proven fact which one verifies on occasion, should the opportunity arise. But you can exist quite well without it, unlike a bank clerk's reliance on ledgers or a cameraman's on pictures. Is it that state of phrenzy which induces a lad to mimic cowboys or an old spinster to converse with her stuffed cat?

The spinster opposite me in the train from Bristol sat severe in black, with an imitation silver brooch on her coat.

Beside her sat a fidgety boy of about ten with a bandaged hand, nervously and jealously watching across the aisle as his father and mother chatted independently on their separate mobile phones with his brother at home. Yes, Cain, we understand your motives, but excuses seem ever thinner. Next to me a potbellied man perspired into a bright red handkerchief which gave the unfortunate impression of being covered in his lifeblood. He seemed to be on the verge of starting conversations, so I took out my battered *Children of Gebelawi* by Naguib Mahfouz, with its old bookmark, a tatty Central Bank of Egypt twenty-five piastre note, worthless outside its country of origin. Anybody would think that the same was true of Mahfouz's ambitious novel, for outside Egypt it has never been understood or appreciated as it would if written by Balzac or Thomas Mann.

'When Qasim's thoughts, passionate desires, and youthful dreams fatigued him, in the shade of Hind's rock, he always allowed his gaze to rest on his sheep's wanderings and playing, their nuzzling affection and sudden squabbles instantly forgotten. He especially loved the innocent antics of the wobbly lambs, and often felt as though they were speaking with him and each other. He contrasted their peaceful life under his guidance with the suffering of the people under their own harsh leaders. Everyone looked down socially on shepherds, but in his heart he knew that shepherds were more honourable than tricksters, layabouts, or beggars.'

My eyes closed, but not before I had noted the minute scrutiny of the woman opposite. I recalled Batty's habit of exchanging cards with men and women casually met in airports, planes, stations and trains. He would offer the unsuspecting victim a card from his cardcase, having previously read the name and address on it, for it would be a card given him by a previous gull. 'Toth Janos, Petroleum Enginner, Hungarian National Oil Enterpris' was one of the selection I had looked at; another was 'Wilbur J. Wallfisch, Investment Consultant, Suite 1298, 184 Madison Avenue, New York'. He would then assume the accent needed, apologising for his strange speech, and filing away the new card he had been handed for a future occasion.

I tried this on my silent interrogator opposite: 'May I introduce myself?', handing her a card once given me by a certain L. J. Gorrage, Radwan Industries, Doha, Qatar. 'I note you have dimples, and very attractive they are too. My own company, Radwan Industries, is concerned with cosmetic technology as applied especially to female hands and face, such as quick tattoos, off-the-shelf moles, and a whole-range of do-it-yourself henna plans. We are currently researching a device, which I may add is confidential but I guess you are a lady of discretion, and can keep whatever you hear under your hat. The purpose to which we are currently devoting our best efforts is the production of new dimples on the face, or the nurture and maintenance of those already in existence. Now it is necessary, our tests have shown, that the cellular tissues surrounding the spot where the dimple is, or will be, should become susceptible to its production by means of massage. This condition is fulfilled by the process which, I may add is confidential, and by the apparatus I represent by this diagram something like a corkscrew or a factory-bench vice. Set the knob here I shall call A of the arm I shall call B on the selected spot of the face I shall call C. Place in position the extension I shall call D and the cylinder I shall call E, then holding the knob I shall call F with one hand, the brace I shall call G is made to revolve on the axis I shall call H. The cylinder E makes a kind of hammered mass of the skin around the spot C.'

'What is the book you are reading, Mr Gorrage?' The imperious voice sounded a mixture between Sybil Thorndike, Edith Evans, and Gertrude Stein.

'It is a novel by an Egyptian writer, in Arabic.'

'I am afraid you are an impostor,' she announced clearly and loudly, so that necks were craned in my direction.

'What do you mean?'

'You are reading the book from right to left. I think you have no more knowledge of Arabic than I. However, I shall let you off if you come and see me in Bath.'

'Where do you live?'

'It is a village in the salubrious environs: we call it Combe Down. My name is Olivia Chart-Palland, of New Simla, 15 Combe Road, next to the New Christian Church.'

'New Simla?'

'We are of old Raj stock, Mr Gorrage. Our family was one of the founders of Boileaugunge, and we were not summer visitors, but residents connected with the Administration. The Chart-Pallands of Somerset were on speaking terms with Lord Curzon. Though *she* was from Chicago, I understand. Do you know Simla, Mr Gorrage?'

'I have never been farther East than the Arabian Gulf.'

'An education, I warrant you, that young men of your age sadly require. I can assure you that I hear now the foxtrot percolating through the open windows of Benmore's ballroom and the dull tap of croquet mallet on croquet ball. I can see the glint of the jampanees' lanterns as they dot about the paths like glow-worms. I can hear the clean clip-clop of horses' hooves on a clear winter morning, and faint cuck-ooo, cuck-ooo somewhere far off. I was champion woman archer, Mr Gorrage, in those shadowy glens, three years in a row.'

'I should like to see your photo album.'

'I fear I have no photos of the jampans. The rickshaws came later, you know, just before they built the railway line from Kalka. I have photos of a rickshaw, with my married sister Geraldine.'

The lines on her face seemed as hard as rubber – my fingers might have bounced off them – but this antique relic of the Raj struck me as lonely, vulnerable, and even after all this time a total stranger in England's strange flatnesses, and garishly-green fields. She would have thought the steep slopes and ravines of the Lower Himalayas the most normal habitat of Man: Mount Olympus, the Abode of the Little Tin Gods. A little to the north of the 31st parallel of latitude and a little to the east of the 77th meridian of longitude, a few leagues merely from the Sutlej.

A great denizen of the ruling class had become an anonymous old lady in black in a nebulous mass of humanity who cared nothing for her memories. Her golden days, scintillating snows, respectful servants – how could she survive so courageously? I am post-war, post-Raj, post-Hiroshima man, relying on nothing but a few exams, experience, connections,

cunning, resourcefulness. She has nothing with which to meet the sneering menaces of my generation except a threadbare pension, maybe a rented or mortgaged bungalow, and persistent dignity. My generation is suspicious of dignity; we treat direct response as a virtue, subtlety as a vice. We do what our novelli Machiavelli tell us, without believing in their authority over us. The gurus of the flower generation have wilted: their amiable marijuana has been stealthily replaced by tremorish cocaine. She and I are alike in choosing not to go out alone at night, here, in England. We tell ourselves the tales of Shahrazad to cheer each other up. The train reassures us by mimicking the illusion of motion: Olivia Chart-Palland is no more fooled by this than I am.

I warm towards her. 'I am staying with a friend in Royal Crescent: Margot Liddell.'

'A Miss Margot Liddell. No, I can't say I've come across the name. Is she a young lady of your own age.'

'Exactly, yes, as a matter of fact.'

'I used to keep a goldfish.'

'Why did you stop?'

'Because it meets the same water back and forth, up and down, and I felt sorry for it, so I took it back to the shop.'

'Do you have a cat?'

'I now have two cats, a white one and a black one.'

'I think you mean a white one and a coloured.'

'I am sure we have a great deal in common, Mr Gorrage.'

'My name is not Gorrage.'

'Precisely. My name is not Chart-Palland.'

'David Quitregard, Lecturer in Arabic at Cambridge.'

'Miriam Blumenfeld, retired trichologist.'

'Trichology?'

'The study and treatment of the hair. You know, dandruff, seborrhoea, and that kind of thing. Baldness. Hair falling out in tufts or handfuls.'

'On the increase, is it, like road accidents?'

'Oh, yes, precisely. More cars, more accidents. More people, more hair, more dandruff, more baldness. The stark simplicity of the increase in incidence is a matter of record.'

'They count the specks of dandruff and divide by the number of people who have it.'

She gurgled farther back in the throat than any laughter I have heard before or since. She patted me on the back of the hand as the train pulled in to Bath Spa, and I reciprocated her charming familiarity by pulling down her case. She had been to stay with an old friend in Clifton whose husband had just died. I was tempted to add that my own father had just died, but I felt it tactless to draw attention to the difference in our ages. Temperamentally, we were close. On an impulse, I decided to wait until tomorrow before seeing Margot and I shared a taxi to Combe Down with the sprightly old lady in black and our two suitcases: mine of battered brown leather, which had suffered long service in Lebanon, and hers of elegant blue, clearly new and showing no signs of wear.

28

The door was opened by Mrs Tax, her tiny, jumpy, miniature housekeeper, who wore the green overalls used by hospital cleaners. Mrs Tax came in for an hour a day when Miriam was at home, and twice a day to feed the cats when Miriam was away. Radio 1 was hammering lunatically in the kitchen. Osbert and Sacheverell, the two fat cats, were on the verge of slumber in the lounge. Miriam gave Mrs Tax a headscarf she had bought in Clifton: Mrs Tax opened it critically, and thought at some length of the correct words to phrase her thanks. 'It's very nice, Mrs Bloomfield, it'll go well with my new brown. Very kind of you to think of me. Is your friend recovering?'

'No. She seems to be shocked by having to do everything instead of only ninety-five per cent.'

'You can't get over it so easy if you've been married a long time. You push a heavy weight along all those years, then suddenly whoosh! It's vanished into thin air. Some women never recover.'

'Ruth will never recover. She's always had someone else to work for. She was the eldest daughter of seven children, and she was almost a mother to the youngest ones from the earliest years she can remember. It's only when it's all over that you don't understand why it was always you who had to do everything. The freedom is turning her neurotic. She is taking the sleeping pills her doctor prescribed for the dead man, her husband. I have a migraine, Mrs Tax. Bring me my Migraleve and let me sleep for a few hours. Make Mr Quitregard a cup of coffee, please.' She turns to me.

'Mr Quitregard, there is a spare bedroom at the back which Mrs Tax will make up for you. If you cannot find your friend in Royal Crescent, you will be welcome to use it.'

'It's awfully kind of you.'

'But I must really go and lie down to cure this headache. Please excuse me.'

'Yes, of course.'

From the kitchen a mysterious mixture of singing, clattering, and chattering was being purveyed by Mrs Tax, like a one-woman concert party. So far accustomed to doing housework on her own, like many ladies (and I noted the first signs in Sophie, too) she told herself what she was going to do, what she was doing, and then, briefly, what she had done. She scolded saucepans for being in the way or hiding in cupboards. She cursed chairs that ambushed her shins, encouraged kettles to boil by talking to them, and laughed about people or events that floated in and out of her head like speedy, insubstantial clouds. I heard her drop a spoon, bang a drawer shut, and nag the kettle for whistling too loudly.

'I've brought you a chocolate biscuit with it,' she said, placing a plastic tray on the lounge table, 'and if there's nothing else, I'll be off. I've got to write up my diary.'

'Your diary?' I enquired dutifully, stirring sugar into the milky coffee.

'It's going to be called "The Diary of an Edwardian Landlady," she said. 'Found a squashed fly on the Sally Lunns, that kind of thing. They say if you do the drawings on the same page, everybody wants to read it. It's not surprising. I find it very interesting myself. Little Dolly Acorn going off with that insurance man from Shepton Mallet. And I know who steals the empty beer bottles from King William IV.'

'Do you know the best way to get to Royal Crescent?'

'I should just think I do. You take a bus from Combe Road to the Bus Station, then walk through. No more than twenty minutes walk.'

'Thanks very much.'

'Bus every fifteen minutes.'

'Splendid.'

'I'll be off, then.'

'Thanks very much for the coffee, Mrs Tax.'

'That's all right.'

She stowed the little paper-wrapped gift into her stout shopping bag, then struggled into her mauve woollen coat, picked up the bag, and with all the determination of a mouse venturing forth from its hole to confront a hostile world she opened the front door, smashed it defiantly closed, and made off left down Combe Road.

The white cat and the black made convulsive movements suggesting both inertia and stretching; they were clearly confederates of long standing: comfortable allies in a world that human beings made absurdly complicated by sudden exits and entrances, sounds and furies. Sacheverell and Osbert exemplified the law of entropy more effectively than any abstraction: and they were beautiful, too, in every way that an artist could imagine. Symmetrical bookends to delight Mondrian; eight splayed limbs to please Jackson Pollock; grave Egyptian sculptures, seated; mischievous Jan Steen adventurers at play; the frozen music of Carpaccio, every hair glinting in bright summer light; immortals shadowy, immobile, in a Rembrandt interior; proudly stalking in a spring garden beside a little girl in pink muslin, as Greuze or Fragonard would have wanted. And yet none of these, for sure, but Rudyard Kipling's cat that walked by itself, never wholly belonging to each other, much less to a human. The only true jungle animal, wild-green of eye and terrible of tail, that we allow to wander freely in our living-rooms.

Finishing my coffee, I nodded to Osbert and Sacheverell and padded quietly up the stairs. I knocked on the front bedroom door.

'Come in,' murmured a weary voice.

'I thought I wouldn't go until I'd seen if you were all right.' In the darkened room a steeple of light from the side of the drawn curtains illuminated an elongated triangle of quilt.

She lay quite still, but I knew she was awake, stiff with the pain I had sometimes seen in my father, who had suffered migraines once a month or so. I sat on the bed tentatively, so as not to hurt her legs, and reached out for her head. Her brow was covered with a folded flannel once wet and cold, now slightly damp but warm. 'I'll get you a fresh cold flannel,' and I went out onto the landing. I relieved myself before putting the flannel under the cold tap, and wondered whether to phone Margot to ask if I could come over. Would she welcome me? I preferred to go unannounced. As Mrs Tax had advised, I should use the bus, and I should come back here if I couldn't stay with Margot.

I took the flannel into the dark front room and felt for her head, which felt dry as parchment, burning, anguished. I pressed the cold gift down, adjusting it by the feel of the fringe of her grey hair, ears, lined cheeks. An enormous tenderness for this formidable old lady surged up in me, and I took gentle hold of her right hand, as it rested palm down on the quilt, squeezing it in sympathy. She responded with a firm squeeze, and raised my hand to her lips for a moment before pressing it down again.

Softly treading downstairs, I was met at the front door by the white cat, tail erect, who wanted to go out. I slipped into my pocket a spare front-door key from the hall table, put on my raincoat, opened the door, and with Osbert (or it may have been Sacheverell) issued forth into Combe Road to await the city bus.

Under my breath I sang, waiting at the moonstruck bus-stop, from Mahler's Song of the Prisoner in the Tower:

Und weil du so klagst, der Lieb' ich entsage!
Und ist es gewagt, und ist es gewagt,
So kann mich nichts plagen!
So kann ich im Herzen stets lachen und scherzen.
Es bleibet dabei, es bleibet dabei.
Die Gedanken sind frei! Die Gedanken sind frei!

By the bus-stop I took out my mobile phone and called Batty's home.

'Hello, Lizzie. Is Batty back from Glasgow yet?'

'Who is this?'

'David. David Quitregard. I just wanted to ask him to phone Newport Post Office when it opens tomorrow, and ask if there's a card on the notice-board for Tithe Barn Antiques. I'll call back tomorrow about the same time.'

'Where are you calling from?'

'Blabichov.'

'What?'

'Sempaditch Dovalong Blabichov. Be in touch tomorrow, Lizzie, ciao.'

The bus drew up, and I fled inside. To Margot!

29

Or at least to the crowded, fume-noxious bus station. By this time it must have been seven and I was hungry, so I stopped off at a fish-and-chip shop in a pedestrian precinct and fortified myself in case I was offered nothing at Margot's.

I ran up Union Street like an escaped thief, then more slowly up the slope of Milsom Street, cantered left along George Street, then pounded up Gay Street into the Circus, where street lights cast their ghostly glows into the great oak dominating the Regency encirclement. From here, according to my street plan, it was a brief jog along Brock Street to Royal Crescent.

Number Seventeen. Up the steps. Where's the bell? Stop your heart thumping: it's only a woman, but what a woman, the raven-haired long-nosed seductress.

An elderly man with a straggly moustache and watery eyes eventually opened the door, without a word.

'I'm looking for an old friend of mine, Margot Liddell.'

'Basement'.

'I beg your pardon?'

He pointed to Hell.

'Down there.' And slammed the door.

I went back into Royal Crescent, then down a steep flight of stone steps, past a barrel for rainwater and a concrete trough listing to starboard, presumably not with the weight of a few listless begonias.

I knocked on the door. It opened.

It was. At last.

'Margot. Do you remember me? I'm David Quitregard, from Cambridge.'

She looked at me and through me in a single comprehensive stare, without a trace of intimacy. Then she opened the door wider, and I walked in. The place seemed like a carefully-restored stage set after a burglary. Everything had been somehow set down in a place not its own. What had happened in the last six years or – even more intriguing – in the last six hours?

Margot was thinner, and more restless than I recalled, apparently on the defensive. A framed photograph of a vaguely-familiar man's face on the stucco mantelpiece. By an 'eighties CD-player I saw records by Tom Jones, Tina Turner, and Shirley Bassey, but no sign of nursing uniform. She was dressed in a blue shirt with old jeans, and wore a wedding-band but no engagement ring. I tried to guess the past, but gave up.

'I tried to contact you at Addenbrooke's but when I called you'd left and they had no forwarding address.'

She still said nothing.

'Eventually I called the library, and they said you were here. From the Nurses' Register. A shot in the dark. How are you?'

'What do you want?'

'I don't want anything, Margot. How are you?' I didn't know whether to approach her, but I warily remembered her tigerish nature, and remained in my chair, placed in such a way as to receive the full draught from the door.

She stood above me, just far enough away to avoid contact by a sudden movement of my arms.

'I gave up nursing for the time being, but I'm still on the Register because I might want to go back.'

'What are you doing?'

'I'm on the dole.' She considered what to say, then: 'Are you staying in Bath?'

'I'm staying with an old lady in Combe Down.'

'D'you want a sandwich?'

'Thanks, I've just eaten, but I could use your facilities.' She showed me the tiny toilet and bathroom. From the neutral interior, so she could reply without showing her feelings, I called out:

'Are you still being chased by octopuses or elephants every night?'

Her reply was non-committal. I took my time flushing the toilet and washing my hands, giving her time to adjust to meeting me again. Who was the man in the photo? I heard a knock on the front door. Margot rushed to me and said 'Stay in there and keep quiet.'

I heard the voice of two women, then the door closed again. Margot was still talking, however. Then she came back and said through the closed door: 'You can come out now.' When I emerged I found a round-eyed little girl of about three looking up at me in wonderment.

'Is it Daddy?' she asked of nobody in particular.

'No, love, Come on, time for bed,' and they went into the bedroom hand in hand.

I mooched around for something to read, but apart from the *Woman's Weekly* and an old *Daily Mail* there was nothing except a faded nursing textbook and a rag-book used to teach infants the alphabet.

155

Margot was back in the room again, her hand still on the door-handle, as if uncertain whether to face me.

'You have a beautiful daughter, Margot. What's her name?'

'Diane.'

I pointed to the photo in the frame. 'Diane thinks I'm like her father.' Again the silence of timidity.

'If you don't want me here, Margot, I'll go away.'

Her eyes filled with the tears so familiar in the pages of *Woman's Weekly*. I was being written into her own story, perhaps the one she had read today: I must remember to read it to find out what I am expected to do next.

'What's the matter, love?' I chose the word she had used for her own daughter. Now it's time to touch her.

'Do you know who that is?'

'The man in the photo? No: who is it?'

'Kit Sweeney. My daughter is called Diane Sweeney. I've gone back to my maiden name. I hated them calling me Mrs Sweeney.' She was in a flood of tears by now, gripping my arms with her hands, and burying her face in my coat, in the approved manner of romantic young ladies. But this was not simply a cliché she had practised in her imagination. This willing victim of chains, taut ropes and leather thongs had fallen in love with – and possibly married, to judge by her ring – one of the three racing-drivers who could have brought the Formula One world championship to Britain. I barely knew the faces of David Coulthard, Martin Brundle and Kit Sweeney, but they must have featured regularly in the sporting magazines and papers, on pages which I never opened.

It gradually wriggled out by a process of question and answer, interrupted convulsively by sobs and tears, that Margot, who hated motor-racing, but went along to Silverstone to watch the Schumacher brothers and Mika Hakkinen in a process of self-chastisement which I had experienced at first hand, had taken the fancy of Sweeney. She had asked for his autograph and he had proposed a date out of the blue. This was a blindingly obvious parody of a woman's magazine story, and the ending was soggily predictable. They had lived together for a few weeks, four years ago, and Diane had been born 'of that union'. He had left her in the same way that he left all his women: the motor-racing circuit was planned in such a way as to make a stable married life totally impossible, and Sweeney was a victim of the circuit no less than Margot herself, or Diane. He took up with a Brazilian girl, a Canadian girl, a South African girl, and two in Italy. 'In Almagna duecento e trentuna', as the saying goes, 'cento in Francia, in Turchia novantuna, ma in Ispagna son già mille e tre'.

She said she had told Kit that getting married was a racing-driver's best insurance, because he would always drive more carefully if he knew there was somebody waiting for him. He agreed, to the opposite effect. That if he knew a woman was anxiously awaiting him, he would drive more carefully and hence more slowly and never win. The purpose of racing was never to take part, but solely to win. Of thirty drivers starting, twenty-nine were already guaranteed to lose, so what conceivable value could there be in placing any more difficulties on a man's track?

'So I said. "Go ahead, then. Go and kill yourself." I don't care. Liddell's Law.'

'What is Liddell's Law, Margot?'

'Two people will always misunderstand each other, if it is possible to do so.'

'And it is always possible.'

She nodded mutely, another abandoned Shahrazad whose peripatetic Sultan had flown on his magic carpet from one seduction to the next.

I recalled how, in a skid at a chicane, Kit Sweeney's car had turned over at Monza two years ago, burning the car and the man's body in a Hell of flames before the firefighting team and ambulance had the slightest chance to reach them.

For the press, it was another occasion to lament an episode in the mediocre course of English motor-racing; another disaster. For the women who patiently awaited their annual weekend alone with a man on easy terms with bewitching Death, that black-clad Shahrazad who lures us with promises of a better life on the other side of today. For those women, I wondered, what can this sight of mangled, twisted, sizzling flesh have meant? That they died too, at that moment? Or that they must find the next man to challenge Fatal Shahrazad, their rival?

Margot kept a portrait of her rented man, but nothing here showed evidence of the daughter he had given her, except a greasy rag-book. I took her hand at last.

'I'd like to help, if you'll let me, Margot.'

'Did you get married?'

I nodded.

'Children?'

I nodded. To speak would irretrievably break the spell of our reunion. She had ruptured one side, but mine was intact, beautiful as a nightingale's song in the smog-grey city. To speak of the intervening years would diminish the magic power of

158

our once true union, based on our once true natures. We could recall our youth six years ago by forgetting the intervening events, accidents, false trails, missed connections. What was real was my masculine whipping, her feminine passion under the sudden thong.

'Her name is Blanche,' I said to my amazement. 'She has copper-coloured hair, and I whip her every night before we go to bed. She always bleeds.'

At last she held up her arms to me, closing her eyes as she always did. But this time, six years on, I was no longer a dominant King David, the clean-limbed hero-doctor who would start a sheep-ranch with her in New South Wales, or a cattle-ranch in Texas. I was a resurrected racing-driver, tiger to her tigress. She went to extinguish the light in her room, her basement, her crescent, her city, her world. She need no longer look on me, a pale avenger from her distant past, but let her vacuous imagination fill with vivid memories of Burt Reynolds, Clint Eastwood, Sylvester Stallone, and they would fuck her.

Except that she did not raise her mouth to be consoled. She held my body close as if for warmth: the consolation was in the warmth.

First of all I tried to kiss her lips, then her hair, but finally I responded to her mood by tightening my grip on her tense body. Gradually she relaxed.

'David, will you come again tomorrow?' A dismissal.

'Yes.' I briefly kissed her forehead, switched on the light by the front door, took my coat, and closed the door behind me without looking back. She was preparing. I was quite prepared.

I emerged into the eighteenth-century Crescent as if on to a Palladian stage, rising from the basement steps as if through a trapdoor. Two lovers, with their backs to me, were gazing down over the parkland, an arm around each other's waist. The moon summoned me upward, to Combe Down. I counted my money under a streetlamp. Seventy-six pounds left. No hotel bill; breakfast provided. I prowled the Circus and Gay Street for a taxi.

30

Combe Road crackled with noise. A girl of sixteen was giggling under a lamppost with two boys, holding up her face to the light at its best angle. Revellers were entering and leaving the pub, King William IV, and honking to get past other cars, badly parked in the narrow street.

At my feet prowled Miriam's black cat, his tail erect and quivering. I let him in with me, and Miriam's white cat ran out with a faint mew. The house seemed as cold as the night, and I sought the private luxury of a hot bath before getting into bed. There was no reason to lock the door, for I thought the only other occupant of the house was the sleeping Miriam. I was wrong. She had been awake when I came in, and came into the bathroom to use the toilet. 'You don't mind, do you?' she said.

She was wearing a pink nightie and brocade slippers in red and gold. Without any makeup, her face, arms, and legs were brown with mottles of blue, violet and purple. The skin was beginning to wrinkle even on the fleshier parts of her arms and legs. She smiled at me with a curious intimacy, so that I astonished myself, not for the first time that day, by saying: 'Would you care to join me in the bath?'

Wordlessly she kicked off the slippers and drew the flimsy nightie above her head, revealing first a thick growth of pubic hair and then thin pendulous tits with enormous nipples. I moved over in the bath, but there was no room for her to lie down on her back, so she lay on her side, with my penis touching her thigh.

'I'm glad your migraine is better, Miriam.'

She said nothing, but her eyes drove a force of awareness like a rock drill into my own. I kissed her, feeling the coarse down on her upper lip, and put my arms round her thin back. She was fifty years older than me, but her beauty was inexplicably attractive. I did not want to imagine her at eighteen, at my age, or even at thirty-eight, with her worldly assumption of arrogant elegance. There was an unflinching power about her, a direct choice: yes. We shall be lovers. Yes: we shall be in love. She did not seek to dominate me by guiding my cock into her wrinkled vagina, but lay still as the water gradually became colder. I caressed her legs, and her furrowed cheeks; her kisses were unresponsively chaste, sometimes watchful, sometimes with eyes closed.

Before I caught cold I got out of the bath and began to towel down. She soon followed, after watching me cover with shirt and boxer shorts.

'I want to spend the night in your bed.'

She did not reply, as if a word might snap her enchantment over me. She led the way, still silent, and got into bed in the dark. I felt her move beside me: she was kneading cream into her nipples and cunt, reviving her juices like a forgotten first wife in an old Sultan's harem.

I became the wilful, unexpected Sultan, caressing her body as she lay back with legs parted and arms perfectly still by her side. When I am forty-eight, she would be in her nineties, I thought incredulously. And still there is this vitality and fascination, this lure of her companionship both spiritual and fleshly. She was stroking my face expertly, remaining as silent as ever, at last allowing me to kiss her lips. I rested my palm above her cunt, then found the clitoris and held it between thumb and index finger, rubbing it gently while she slid her dextrous hand along my rod as it heated and thickened. 'I love you, darling Miriam,' I was saying. She wriggled down the bed and lodged her head between my legs. I raised the sheet so she would not suffocate, running my fingers down her spine as she sucked deeply. I kissed her back as she brought me to climax. Far into the night we kissed and clung like desperate raftborne drifters on a dangerous sea, terrified that each moment would be our last.

She had loved before, of course, but all those previous passions were subsumed in this, our finding of each other. I talked to her of vows, truth, faithful days and nights, the waking into awareness of her beauty, and nothing, nothing she said for good or ill, as if one word might sever the subtle cobweb surrounding us.

There are two kids of magic in Islam: Rahmani (Compassionate, Divine, as Rahman is one of the many names of Allah), and Shaitani (Diabolical). Perfection in Rahmani consists in the knowledge of the most great name of God, al-Ism al-'Azam, a knowledge imparted to the few favoured by Heaven. Perfection in Shaitani is provided by the Devil and his evil spirits. Enchantment is almost always evil, but throughout the history of man it is acknowledged that some Rahmani magicians have invoked genies for good and lawful purposes, and here in this bed I felt possessed as a victim of such Rahmani magic.

I felt the skin and bones of Miriam as if they were the voluptuous limbs of a showgirl; I kissed her thin lips as if they were the full and fragrant lips of Blanche Afanasian. Her expectant silence appeared as eloquent as Rose Calder's vibrant sex words. Even her cats' green eyes opened round crystal globes of fiery desire. I might *want* to think about Margot Liddell, but I couldn't: my whole being was suffused with the ecstasy of Miriam's presence. I told her that I wanted to make love to her all day and all night: that she inflamed all my senses and my mind. We were not a man and a woman but a whole person, serene yet never immobile in that integral bond. To 'Do you love me, Miriam?' there was no answer. 'Do you love me, Miriam, as I love you?' We slept.

31

I awoke in the morning to the dreary flap flop of rainwater dripping from the eaves. I had a severe headache, and went downstairs – after slipping on my trousers – to ask for Panadol. Miriam was washing up at the kitchen sink at the back of the house. The cats were asleep, their saucers empty. Miriam had breakfasted. It was nine o'clock. I kissed her but at that moment I swear I couldn't remember any of the details of what I had said and done the night before clearly enough to mention them or describe them. All I remembered was that Miriam herself had for some reason said nothing. Now she avoided looking me straight in the face. Was it to avoid repeating the sequence of the day before, or embarrassment, or disgust at my behaviour or at her own? I would be curious to know, even now.

'What do you want for breakfast?'

I should have said, 'Nothing, I want to spend the day in your arms,' but I said, 'Whatever you care to make. I'm not fussy.'

I tried to avoid looking at her curved back and shoulders, and the awkwardly slow movements of her legs. But I saw. All the same, I saw. The blue veins in the back of her hands, the impatience in the old movements as the white cat slithered between her legs, yailing for food. The black cat watched developments, like an experienced terrorist allowing his hotheaded younger comrades to taste fear in their mouths. Scalding fat from the frying-pan spilt on to the cat, a split second before it howled and darted away.

Miriam was not yesterday's lover, eloquently silent in the stirring forest, but just saying nothing, as if emptied of words by a tremendous event. The old are less capable of absorbing traumatic change; they resist it. Miriam looked tired of resisting.

'Would you like to go out?' I asked cheerfully, as if not understanding her pallid fatigue.

'There,' she said, 'I forgot to buy mushrooms. Is that enough?'

'That is magnificent. Thank you, my dear.' Too patronising. I must not wound her: then, after last night most remarks will seem part of a cruel anti-climax.

I decided to change the subject altogether.

'But what if I were not a Lecturer in Arabic at all? What if I were a blind seamstress in a Paris garret, a child still buried alive in a Mexican earthquake, a pastoral shepherd in Kazakhstan once ruled by Russians but unable to understand a word of their language? What if I were a bird, a cosmonaut, the planet Jupiter? Yes, all right. I'm a Lecturer in Arabic, but elusive enough to be a merchant seaman in Pattaya, or an industrialist in Chicago. An actor refuses diminishing to a single rôle, so why shouldn't I?'

She considered her reply. 'That is very good for you.' And with a heavy irony, 'Congratulations.'

'You mean, I am lucky to have so many options possible, to live in a free country, in peacetime, and be a member of an unpersecuted majority?'

'It is very good for you. That you do not have anyone who depends on you. Nobody relies on you. That is what I mean.

My father in Danzig had twelve people relying on him. He was not a lecturer, nor a cosmonaut nor a pastoral shepherd. He was a doctor, and with my mother, his two sisters, an old deaf uncle, and eight children he should have had a little bit of spare time. But to earn enough money he worked every morning and every afternoon except on Saturdays when he took a walk by the seashore or in the country. In the evenings he taught a Polish boy German, except when he was called out by a patient. At nights he studied, or read or slept, unless he was called out by a patient. He died at the age of forty-five: a doctor. It is very good for you. But not so good, not so good for him.'

She sat down because she had upset herself with her own story. She had not considered that my story might have been concocted to make her feel better. For her, at her age, memories were too weighty, too tentacular to fend off with a night's passion. If she were to reward me with the devotion of every single night of the rest of her life, I should remain a stranger from dawn till dusk, beating in vain on her family's door in Danzig. I had been born four decades too late, in the wrong country. She was more distant from me than from her father, the good doctor. She might allow me the right to her frail, aged body, but to whom were her thoughts returning as she touched me? During those dark silences, those hours of physical nearness, what gulf of horrors separated my last word from her first? Sixteen at the outbreak of the Great War, she would have been twenty-two at its end. How had she left Danzig, and when? What had she to do with Treblinka, with Langfuhr now called Wrzeszcz, with the Reich Labour Service? Did she bid people 'Auf Wiedersch'n!' or 'Do widzenia!'?

She had rejected me, as a professor might reject the advances of a go-getting undergraduate with her eye on a reputable First. Perhaps she thought I intended to steal for myself a few of those extraordinary memories that are the exclusive preserve of the old, or of the great explorers: Shackleton, Freya Stark, Nansen, Charles de Foucauld, Wilfred Thesiger: that strange and radiant community that must despise office-workers in Atlanta or Swindon, for their time is of a different dimension, as St Catherine's in Sinai is of a different dimension from St John's, Blinco Grove. The pilgrim's effort to attain it makes St Catherine's ethereal. Like the isolation of the Coptic Cathedral in Muslim Cairo, where threats of fire-raising and petrol-bombing are routine. It is dangerous to be a Jew in Benghazi, a Christian in Mecca, now a Muslim in New York ... Yet what is a conformist's view worth anywhere?

I had to persist. 'Would you like to go out?'

'I should be taken for your aunt,' she answered, as if she had given the matter great thought. Why not then 'mother'?

'I'll spend the day in Bath on my own, then. Shall I leave my case here?' She looked directly at me, like a bold girl on being asked for her first date.

'No,' she replied, as if taking into account what her parents would say if they knew. What was happening now, a disintegration, followed as plausibly and fatefully as what had happened in her bathroom and bedroom the night before. She was surrendering passionate days, weeks, months, years, perhaps the rest of her life, on a caprice. Did she not trust me? Did she trust herself? Were the lonely years too precious to abandon: a solitary certainty better than the quandary of meeting, loss, quarrels, parting? Perhaps she was not tough enough to accept the inevitability that she would die before me. Or was it that the divorce proceedings and remarriage would have humiliated her, as everyone pointed the finger of derision at her, December trapping April?

I felt for her too keenly to enquire her motives; instead I packed my case, used her toilet, put on my coat, waved to

Osbert and Sacheverell, and then kissed Miriam passionately on the lips once again before opening the door, and shutting it quickly behind me. The bus was just coming.

32

At the terminus I took my case over the road to the rail station, and checked it in at the Left Luggage Office. I could hardly arrive in Royal Crescent with it, under the eye of that brigadier with the straggly moustache and watery eyes.

At the station I bought a Bounty bar with a pound coin for the 10p pieces in change, and called Newport Post Office.

'Hi gmarnin, this is NBC in Waashington. The Noose Service would like to ascertain whether you have a notice up for Tithe Barn Antiques.' (Rustle, whisper, giggle.) 'No? Well, thanks anyway. Have a nice day.'

Dull, overcast, Bath was preparing to shed its coachloads with its leaves, the last of the package tours loafing, unmistakably yet inexplicably lost between the Roman Baths and the Abbey, which are adjacent. Two women outside a bookshop in Milsom Street were noisily exchanging addresses in Omaha, Nebraska and Portland, Maine. 'No, I don't know the Terbrugghens, but I know some De Burghers.' 'Well, now, I declare.'

I sat on a seat in the Circus, gazing down narrow Gay Street and planning for my meeting with Margot. Flowers? Sweets for little Diane? The new *Woman's Weekly*? I decided

170

on flowers, and retraced my steps towards the centre until I came to a florist's. 'A dozen red roses, please.' 'Mm, yes, with the ferns.' 'And a gift card with roses.' I wrote: 'Ever yours. D.' as she wrapped them in cellophane, then pink and white striped paper with 'Interflora' printed on it. And sweets for Diane. Margot had always liked Smarties. I bought two giant tubes of Smarties at a newsagent's.

The rain had started as I entered Royal Crescent, passing number One, then pacing between the cracks on the pavement compulsively, superstitiously, as I had done in childhood. Seventeen. Down to the basement. Knock. No answer. Knock. No answer. I try the handle. It is open. I call 'Margot. David.' No answer. There is the portrait of Kit Sweeney, her Tom Cruise of the race-track. No Margot. A *Woman's Weekly*. A local free newspaper. No Diane. I look outside: the milk bottle is still there. I bring it in, and take it through to the kitchen. I look in the bedroom.

Margot, asleep. No, she raises her head from the pillow. She is wearing the same blue shirt she was wearing last night.

'Whayawan?'

'Margot.' I bend down to kiss her uncombed black hair, and her red lips but her breath is powerful as a sledgehammer. It is neat whisky. I look under the bed: nothing. A bump under the covers: there, a corked bottle, three-quarters empty, its golden residue swilling like urine in a sample-bottle.

'Margot. What's wrong?'

I unbutton her shirt, unhook her bra, kiss her breasts as she is propped up on one elbow: they hang heavy and desired. She flops back on the pillow, and her warm mounds of flesh grow wet under my wandering tongue. Does she remember the torment she enjoyed? Has she a rope or whip? Her jeans are

171

undone already as though she has been contenting her lust in private. I fill her cunt with two then three probing fingers. She lies still, without response. She is stunned by the whisky. I slap her face gently, but she merely turns it away from me. This is not the homecoming I had longed for. I take a jug from the kitchen, filled with cold water, and throw it at close range across her face.

'You bastard!' she pants through the drenching. 'You bastard!' 'You bloody prick!'

'I've brought you a dozen red roses, Margot.' She started to punch my face and chest, but I held her feeble arms by the wrists and she sagged back limply. 'And a tube of Smarties.'

I handed her one of the two cigarettes left in the packet beside the congested ashtray, and lit it. I knew it relaxed her, and I gambled.

'Where's your whip, Margot?'

She blew smoke in my face and grimaced.

'You bastard! I know you, you're fucking Quitregard. Get out of my house!'

'I came to give Diane her Smarties.'

'You came here last night. You're a fucking agent of the DHSS, aren't you?'

'Are you on the dole, Margot?'

She started to laugh, a dirty, cheap, prostitute's laugh, hinting at how she increased the state's provisions for a single parent, a family supplement, an unemployment payment.

'No. I don't do it for money, you bastard, if that's what you think.' Liddell's Law.

I tried to look as though I hadn't thought any such thing. She closed her eyes again, pretending I had gone away.

'Look, Margot, get dressed and we'll go out and get some fresh air.'

'I can't go out. I never go out. The social worker takes Diane out, but I can't face it.'

'Never?'

She giggled. 'There's racing cars out there that mow you down and burn themselves up, with the drivers inside. You wanna be careful, Mr Quitregard, don't stand near the kerb, don't look both ways, don't cross the road. Whatever you do, *don't cross!*' She had screamed the last words, trying to stuff the sheet in her mouth, while I held the whisky bottle away, out of sight, on the floor by the side of the bed. She threw the cigarette away because it had burned her fingers. I went to stub it out with my heel on the faded carpet.

'I don' wanna see those people out there. They hate me. Have you ever seen those people in Royal Crescent? They hate me. They hate each other. They'll hate you. Don' go near them.'

'Margot, if you don't want to go out into Bath, we'll go to Wells. You can lean on me, and we'll wake up together. Then we'll go to bed together tonight, and I'll make you all warm and loved, like I held you last night.'

'Last night? She retorted, suspiciously.

'Before I left I held you tight. Like the old days.'

I had won her over. I left a note for the social worker explaining why I had taken Margot out into the terrifying world, and asking her to keep Diane company until we returned. I initialled it and we made preparations by choosing Margot's wardrobe. I rubbed her face clean with soap and flannel, but her tousled hair remained a mess. I tried brushing it but she snatched the brush out of my hand and started, faltering very soon, and dropping the brush on the floor.

She was giving up in front of the framed Sacred Heart of Jesus pinned on the door, and visible as we looked into her mirror together. She blenched at it: she really still believed in the Catholic teachings of damnation or redemption, and saw herself in the charnel-house, her spirit flickering scarlet, black, scarlet, whitened in the flames that do not devour but eternally chastise. The Jesuit Fathers had seized her conscience, nagging about it, stressing it, repeating its vulnerability, nagging about her susceptibilities, reminding her of the temptations of the flesh. And then what did you do? My dear? She had left the confessional chastened but ever more inquisitive, desirous, open to suggestion, avid.

I and others like me must have seemed companionable devils incarnate with whom she could encompass ecstasies on the way to suffering the torments she would ultimately endure. Unsure of the dogmas, too frightened to go back into the churches, she retained only smudged recollections about teachings concerning the sins of this world and the terrors of the next. Incapable of visualising that white vision of Heaven, that celestial canticled wedding-cake of veils, tiers, and pale uplifted angels' wings towards ineffable, blinding brightness, Margot had long ago given up any attempt at the inaccessible, lavish party for the cardinals, archbishops, and the wealthy. Her place was in the smoky pits, where bits of tyre-rubber lay scattered and the fumes hung rancid among desperate shouts, urgency, in the frenetic desire to roar away in order to … She could not bring herself to realise that the desire was to come back again here to the same place as quickly as possible in order to leave as quickly as possible. In order to finish the whole race as quickly as possible. So that preparation might start as quickly as possible for the next race. And the next season. And the next, *sans fin, sans commencement*. In my beginning is my end: the real banner over the entrance of the nether place. I am the alpha and the omega. I, Margot, I too. Remember how we met, and must meet again now, and must continue to meet for I am your alpha and omega.

🐚 33 🐚

Margot sat still on her bathroom stool, looking vacantly into the mirror, as if she could not understand the principle of mirrors. She did nothing. Like the Dowayo of Cameroon, who have beer, freedom, self-respect and sex (not necessarily in that order) and seldom *do* anything at all. Activity is an invention of Western society. The Greeks thought and taught. The Romans sought and fought. The rest of us bought. And all this time, the Dowayo have chosen to copulate, drink beer, and occasionally tell each other stories. Margot was living on the wrong continent.

But I couldn't tell her so. I pleaded with her to get dressed. Diane had been taken out by the social worker because Margot refused to go out at all. In a revolving nightmare, her elephants were trumpeting again, thundering towards her, their huge muddy legs lumbering into her, trampling every limb, thudding her into unconsciousness, killing her at night, and then by day. Her whisky bottles made sure of their prodigious, total triumph. Between the murders and suicides of the racing-track's eternity ring, Margot had always put up with the hordes of rampaging elephants making for her head, thighs, belly. They raped her, killed her, and rampaged on, round the endless savannah track that led ineluctably back to her body, resurrected (oh yes, in bloody mash and fragments, but alive and suffering) resurrected right enough but only in order that the agony could start again, her body again lying in the centre of the track, not quite mangled enough to satisfy the Father Confessor who would have his last ounce of flesh, the last bouncing, flailing bones, the last fleck of blood on the windscreen.

'I can't go out. I've nothing to wear.'

I found her a good cream suit, but she laughed and put it back, placating me by finding for herself a black blouse and the old jeans she had been wearing yesterday. I took a belt out of the wardrobe and flicked it across her naked buttocks, but she was hardly conscious of it, slipping into her blouse, then her panties, jeans, and finally a pair of open sandals.

She grinned at me. 'Take me out, Mr Man.'

Did she remember who I was? I kissed her.

'Call me David Quitregard.'

'I can't say that.'

'Say it.'

'Daily Kit-e-Kat.'

'David.'

'Davie Kit-e-Kat.'

'Quitregard.'

'Kitty Kit-e-Kat. Davie Kitty Kit-e-Kat.' She laughed, at first snorting then hysterically. I slapped her face.

'Tomorrow we'll be sober, my girl, and today too.' I marched her out of the door, which locked behind us. She clenched her body as the relatively bright light threatened her.

'I can't stand all this air, and all these buildings and people.'

'Of course you can. I'm with you. There's no need to worry. The nightmares are in your head. Out here I'm going to show you that nobody wants to hurt you. You can sit down in the Circus ...'

'What Circus?'

'The round square at the end of Brock Street. Under the spreading chestnut tree. You know the old song. We'll sit down and watch the prams go past with little babies inside.'

'Where's Diane?'

'You told me: out with the social worker.'

'I want her.'

'You can have her, after we've been out to see how nice everywhere looks. This is autumn, in England, season of mellow fruitfulness.'

'You mean, season of fruity bellowmess. I mean mellowness.'

'As you say, melon of beastly fruitiness.'

She giggled, so I must have struck a chord from the past.

She hung closely on my arm as we turned from New Bond Street into High Street, and made our way past the Abbey into Pierrepont St.

At the rail station we stood in line, Margot tense and palely silent at my side. 'Two returns to Wells, please.'

'No,' answered a pimpled youth with ginger whiskers.

'I said, Two returns to Wells, please.'

'No, I'm sorry.'

'Why not?'

'We're not selling tickets to Wells.'

'Whyever not? Is there a strike?'

'No.'

'Have you cancelled all the trains?'

'No.'

'Then why can't we have two tickets to Wells?'

'Because we're not selling tickets to Wells.'

'Why not?'

'Because no trains are going to Wells.'

'Why not?'

'Because there's no railway line to Wells.'

'Eh?'

'There is no station in Wells.'

'Why didn't you say so?'

'I am saying so. I just told you. Next, please.'

Margot was swaying with repressed laughter, thinking I was putting on a comic act for her amusement, or I was an object of rare fun for not knowing that Bath and Wells were not connected by rail.

'Y'll 'ave to go by bus, love,' said a patient woman in a beige coat just behind us, hugging a pekinese which was rolling its eyes at the show. 'The bus station's just across the road, you can't miss it.'

Margot was responding by now to the adventure of a blustery autumn day, truancy from school, her day off from the hospital wards, an opportunity to lose the worries about Diane, elephants, Kit Sweeney and his engulfing flames. It was clear that she thought our smart new coach was about to crash into every oncoming vehicle, every parked car, every bollard, roundabout, overhanging tree, so I tried to distract her with I-Spy with my little eye, who would be the first to see sheep, cows, horses, rabbits. I always let her win, and she clutched my hand in the manner of a favourite niece. Gusts of wind blew gnarled branches on to the coach's roof or windows: these terrors often made her bite her knuckles or wince. She fidgeted constantly, holding the knees of her jeans down with the outstretched palms of her hands or nestling her head on my shoulder, then springing alert at a squeal of braking or the sudden appearance of a car heading straight towards us round a corner.

'No ideas but in things,' said William Carlos Williams. How amply proved in Margot's case. Her every idea was wrapped up in the horror of things, which sprang out at her or lay in wait to snap their jaws, or trampled down her helpless body in its own blood.

The bus dropped us off by a swimming-pool in Princes Road. I was starving by this time and headed for the town centre, dragging Margot, who had never been to Wells and suddenly found a kind of crazed curiosity about these new surroundings.

'Oo, look, at the Regal, they've got *Breakfast at Tiffany's* again this week, and *The Parole Officer* next week. D'you want to go to the pictures?' Had she forgotten me again?

'Maybe, Margot. Let's get something to eat.'

Past the South West Electricity Board she found the old Palace Theatre, with stained-glass announcements for Varieties – Plays – Theatre – Turns – Pictures. Now 'Self-Sufficiency Supplies', the old Palace still had the old beams and girders, bare, exposed like the fashionably plain pine furniture. How to make a rabbit hutch, how to run a strawberry farm, how to make your own beer, how to churn milk: instruction manuals, pots, pans, machinery, gadgets, celebrating an escape from urban routine more momentous than from any Colditz, because it was happening all over England. Inner cities had been taken over by rioting mobs in Brixton, Tottenham, Handsworth, Toxteth: the chain of ugly names for places stranded between pride and demolition. City dwellers were taking refuge in the Arthurian England of Glastonbury and Mells, Shepton Mallet and Priddy.

I dragged Margot past The Good Earth Licensed Restaurant and Wholefood Store over the road to La Bella Napoli for a pizza. She was happy, once across the crowded street, confined in a room at a small table in a small chair. Back to the nursery.

I told her nursery rhymes, which she joined in. I told her I once knew a woman so elegant that she had learnt how to eat celery with dignity; a man whom I knew was a criminal because he stirred his sugar so hard in his coffee that he destroyed all the evidence of its sweetness; and a woman so houseproud that her dusters never got dirty.

After lunch I took her through the crowded Market Place into the Cathedral and we stood before the fourteenth-century inverted arches that support the massive tower. Margot's attention strayed from pillar to pillar, as if she were looking for something.

'Is it the fruit stealers, Margot?'

'Is what the fruit stealers?'

'Are you looking for the capitals carved with the men stealing fruit from the orchard who are beaten by the farmer?'

'No. I was looking at the stone. All these pillars, arches, all the weight of it. Holding everything up, straight. So it doesn't fall down.'

I thought of the lines from Abu 'l-'Ala:

Ka annak al-jism aladhi huwa surat,
Lak fi 'l-hayat fahadhiri an tukhd'a,
La fadl li 'l-qadah aladhi istauda'tahu,
Daraban wa lakin fadluhu li 'l-mauda'i.

'The body, which gives you form in life,
Is but your cup. Be not deceived, my soul!
Cheap is the vessel you store honey in,
But precious for the contents of the bowl!'

Margot had found the mechanical clock, and was watching in fascination as hands and figures moved once more, as they had for nearly six centuries. I showed her embroideries, misericords, and the carved capitals in the south transept.

She murmured by the votive candles, priced at 20 pence each, 'When the pricker stand is full, place your candle in the basket. It will be lit for you later.' She fumbled in her handbag for money, but I forestalled her by slipping a 20-pence coin into the slot, and handing her a candle. The pricker stand was not yet full. She stabbed her candle into a pricker, though she had not lit it. I removed another candle, almost amorphous by now, and lit Margot's candle from it, replacing the old stump in its exact former place.

We pored over tombstones in the cloister wall, and I showed her the moat, where swans approached anxiously for crumbs.

She led me, pulling, back to the tomb plaques and read them out:

'Margaret Isabella Sherston, wife of Peter Sherston Esquire, & only Daughter of Peter Burrell of the Town of Lincster M.D. died the 6th of April aged 29.'

'Sacred to the Memory of Margaret Sherston, second wife of Peter Sherston Esquire of this City and youngest daughter of Thomas Strangeways Esquire of Shapwick in this County. In all amiable Qualities and the Christian Virtues a Pattern to her Sex, Much lamented by not a Few: By a loving Husband and three Children, heavily deplored, After a lingering and painful Illness, which proved a distinguished Piety and exemplary Fortitude, She died on the 10th of January 1795, Aged 39.'

'Peter Sherston, died August 14th 1820, aged 75.'

I took her hand again, and led her back through the cathedral into Vicars' Close, with its old library transformed into a tiny chapel at the end of the apparent cul-de-sac. There she screwed herself up to pray, crossing herself as she had done before every chapel in the Cathedral. Nobody else disturbed her tiny hint of prayer. I stood back, literally and metaphorically, as she approached the personless altar. 'Sanctus Sanctus Sanctus' chanted the altar-cloth, gold on maroon. In an earlier age she would have become a nun, praying at dawn, scouring steps, praying, gardening, cooking, praying, defecating with a blush, praying, laundering, eating, praying, sleeping and dreaming of soft flesh touching hers, gentle fingers, tender voices, sinning, praying.

Margot of the raven hair had bowed her head, but she no longer knew to whom or about what she was praying. Even a nunnery is no longer a redoubt against thieves of conscience, vandals desecrating silence, the roar of inner cannon. Little Bo Peep has lost her sleep, and doesn't know where to find it ...

I shall shelter this waif in my arms until she has found a candle, a flickering iota, of steady reassurance in alleys spreading, diverging in gloomy mists away from her beginning. She retreats backwards, not towards me, but slightly away from me, in the direction of the door. She opens the door, looking obliquely between me and the altar. She darts out and slams the door, pressing against it so I can't get out. But the door opens inwards, so I flick up the catch and away after her. She is running, running, but wayward, stumbling, she falls against a bike someone has left outside their front gate. She has grazed her knee; spots of blood form and ooze out. I unlatch the low gate of the house in Vicars' Close and knock on the door.

What if it is Batty, still chasing Blanche Afanasian? A dumpy woman with a vacuum-cleaner answers the door. 'Yes?'

'Could you help me? First aid? My wife has collapsed in the road and hurt her knee.'

The woman came out, closed her door carefully and bent down to look at Margot, who was sobbing.

'You wait there', she told me, as if expecting her home to be raided by a burglar and his accomplice. 'I'm getting antiseptic and an elastoplast.'

She wouldn't allow Margot in to lie down and rest, but I thanked her for her attention, and held Margot close, as she limped, hopped, and hobbled across Cathedral Green and back to the bus stop.

Margot sulked on the bus journey home, not opening her mouth to speak to me, but occasionally flexing her leg, groaning as if *in extremis*.

'It's just a scratch, love.'

Back at Bath bus station by four-thirty, I phoned up Corinne at the Faculty, but nobody answered; Lizzie for any news of Batty, but a new Swedish au pair answered and said very carefully and distinctly that Mistress Mac Man was not to pee disturbed; and Newport Post Office, asking on behalf of Senator Al Gore whether a card had been tacked up to advertise Tithe Barn Antiques. Nothing but giggles.

Margot was squashed up in a corner, trying to look at nothing and no-one. A soldier with a cigarette was sizing her up salaciously.

'Shall we take a taxi back to Royal Crescent?' Would she like that?

'Mm,' she nodded vacantly. BATH WIDOW MURDERED was a newspaper headline scrawled in black on a white sheet advertising in red the local paper. SPECIAL PROPERTY FEATURE was another. I found a taxi and we headed north up the shallow Avon valley towards Royal Victoria Park. PARK GANG RAPE, I thought. SCHOOLGIRL VIOLATED. Was Diane all right?

'I want to go to bed,' said Margot, with her eyes closed, her head lolling in the corner of the taxi, as we swerved around another bend.

Two women were standing by Margot's door, with a little girl not Diane.

I helped Margot to the door, and pushed it, but it was locked. I remembered: I had closed it this morning without looking for a key.

'Where's your key, Margot?'

'In my handbag.'

'Excuse me for interrupting,' said a plain lady in thick spectacles who looked like a refugee from a home for battered women.

'Where's your handbag?'

'But we're students of the Bible, and I wondered if you could spare us a moment of your valuable time.'

'Probably in the bedroom.'

'Did you know that millions now alive will never die?'

'Is there a window I can force?'

'Do you live here?' piped up the little girl, about ten or eleven.

'No,' I said.

'Do you believe in Armageddon?' insisted the plain woman. 'Have you read the Bible?'

'Margot, where's Diane?'

'She's out with the social worker until lunch-time.'

'Ma, this man's trying to break into someone else's house.'

'But it's five hours since lunchtime, Margot. Where would she be if she weren't here?'

Around the corner of Royal Crescent, in full cry, came a policewoman, the determined social worker I had seen the day before, with Diane in her arms and a police sergeant with a walkie-talkie.

An American woman with a large pink coat, pink hat and blue veil was pointing down to the begonias in troughs in the basement and saying 'Look down here, Sumner, ain't that cute?' At the foot of the steps, Margot had slumped wearily, eyes closed, clutching her plastered knee and sullenly listening to a woman in black telling her about Armageddon, while another severe woman with an anxious child was pointing accusingly up at me. I, poised for flight at the head of the stairs, added up a series of unlikely catastrophes on the fingers of my rapidly confusing brain and did what a rat would have done, or let us be charitable and say a mouse, in the similar circumstances of a ship, if not sinking, then at least heading towards an iceberg sharper and infinitely larger than itself. I whistled a happy tune, and vaulted over the railings into the Royal Victoria Park. There, in the anonymity of hooligans, lovers, peeping toms, willing virgins, men in greasy overcoats, vandals and drug-addicts, there, I say, I felt at home at last. My fingers touched a comforting wad of five ten-pound notes, and the thin but substantial wafer of a left-luggage ticket which would allow me to reclaim my suitcase, and head eastward to London. If, indeed, there was still a station in London. A fat man in braces assured me that there was as he handed over the ticket in exchange for notes of the realm. Change at Paddington. Trains to Cambridge from Kings Cross or Liverpool Street.

'Say goodbye to Pat, say goodbye to Jack,' I waved to the ticket-clerk with my free hand, 'and say goodbye to yourself, because you're a nice guy.'

'So you are, man,' wheezed a Rastafarian cordially, as I opened the door and he step through.

🐾 34 🐾

The train journey from Liverpool Street to Cambridge, quite late, when all the commuters have disappeared, is a secret-service exploit. Some of the young men are Apostles, whether in tweeds or dog-collar. Some of the gruff men with *The Times* and umbrellas are businessmen in the City getting off at Audley End or Bishops Stortford. Some of the shy or morose girls are not up at all, but turn out to be foreign-language students returning after a day shopping in Oxford Street. Some of the relaxed women, with *Good Housekeeping* or *The Guardian*, you realise were at pro-Tibetan independence rallies, or evening recitals at West Road Concert Hall, whenever the Master of Selwyn throws open his adjacent grounds during the long interval for coffee and sandwiches, or strawberries and cream in the season. Some, but not all. Every third or fourth passenger is a mystery, never seen before or after. A Finnish phrase-book sticks out of a pocket. An old trunk with faded Orient Express labels at the end of a compartment seems to belong to nobody: you never see it handled or removed, yet it is gone when you look again. A woman with a lorgnette emerges suddenly from a toilet but the metal shutter still shows 'engaged'. Above you, in the rack too

small for luggage, lies a copy of *Izvestia* with three pages torn out. You overhear words like 'Querétaro' and 'obnounce'. Pocket chessboards abound. The children are quiet, sallow, experienced. A viola-case is handled so lightly that you are certain there could be no viola within. The journey is so flat that Dutch travellers are convinced they are not abroad at all. If you glance up from your Mutanabbi or Sonallah Ibrahim, you can see Gladstone disappearing to the next carriage Metternich, Lord Chesterfield, Clemenceau. There is a whiff of Chanel before the stale smell of jailhouse sweat overpowers it. Bulldog Drummond used this train regularly; once, Ivy Compton-Burnett. It is a Biographers' Special, for bespectacled chain-readers between the British Library in Bloomsbury and Cambridge University Library. Nobody admits to having heard of Royston or Ashwell and Morden. An old whitehaired man with a pipe once sat down opposite me and, as the train was pulling out of Liverpool Street station, reached down under the seat and fetched from the grimy recesses a pair of slippers, which he put on in place of his patent-leather shoes. He told me he was the personal assistant in London to the rightful king of Bulgaria. His son had hired himself out to the Bulgarian secret police as an assassin in Western Europe. It was only a matter of time, puffed the elegant little man contentedly in his bedroom slippers, before his masked son would raid the Madrid mansion where his bearded master resided in constant fear of his life, not knowing whom to trust. Now that same ex-king has become Prime Minister of Bulgaria as Simeon Saxe-Coburg-Gotha.

I recognised a tall lady as the world's leading authority on cuneiform, the Assyrian hatchet-tongue, when she constantly exchanged pages covered with coded axes, as her eyes tired with the train's motion, for knitting needles and coded instructions for purling and plaining.

A cabinet minister, a Queen's Messenger, two merchant bankers, an episcopal aide-de-camp, a contralto: as I walked through the train few of them looked up, for they saw this train-ride as an intermezzo between discussions and arguments: a necessary grace after work and before eating. Borrowed moments they would never be called upon to repay, like a blank page in last year's diary.

I knew I had to invent characters, times and dialogue, trialogue, polylogue, for Sophie, about Glasgow and the Seminar. I carefully removed from my pockets, like a canny Professor Moriarty, all traces of Bath and Wells, like a restaurant bill, four bus tickets. My shirt was too dirty, with a three-day deposit of dirt on collar and cuffs, but I could blame that on Glaswegian muck.

I had chats with Neil Strutt, Harbick, and Leggate to report, but I should have to create a realistic legend about lectures and conversations I had neither heard nor overheard. I could throw Sophie off balance by asking her about her days without me, the boys, and her parents the Summerburns, their weather, their alsatians.

35

But when I arrived home, hungry again, in a station taxi, none of that mattered at all. Because somebody had phoned Sophie; she wasn't saying who it was, man or woman, but someone had told her I had not been at the Seminar all the time, or not in Glasgow all the time. I couldn't ask her who it was, in case it emerged I had been seeing more than one woman.

I kissed her on arrival, but she drew away from my touch.

'Where are the boys?'

'Don't you touch those boys. They're in bed.'

'Why can't I touch them?'

'How do I know you haven't been seeing other women on all these Seminars that you go to?'

'What other women?'

'And then sneaking back here with the milk float.'

'What milk float?'

'You know!'

'I swear to you I don't know what you're talking about.'

'It's in the local paper. Look at that. PETERHOUSE DAIRY. Sir John Thomas was not amused when he came down to breakfast today to find a Dairy Crest milk float instead of his dining-table in the Master's Lodge of Peterhouse in

189

Trumpington Road. Apparently, a nocturnal intruder had dismantled the milk float, hauled the bits in by the window while the Master was sleeping, and reassembled them before dawn, leaving the way he came. The only clue to the prankster's identity is a message in Scrabble letters rearranged from letters in his name to form an anagram. College and university lecturers are helping with suggestions to solve the anagram, but when we went to press their efforts had not met with success. The message ran D DID GIVE R A RAQUET. Workmen from Peterhouse have spent the rest of the day, with representatives of Dairy Crest, discovering how to take the milk float to pieces in order to restore order in the dining-room at Sir John's Lodge.

'I don't get it.'

'Who do you know in the university who plays real tennis with a raquet?'

'Dozens of people.'

'And has a town crier's uniform ...'

'Um'.

'Who did you play with last?'

'Um. I think it was Batty. Of course it's his town crier's outfit.'

'Exactly,' she said with heavy irony. 'D for David, R for ...'

'Oh come on now, I know his name is Bartholomew but everybody since schooldays has called him Batty.'

'And I suppose everyone knows you as David Quitregard.'

'Of course they do.'

'So when they work out the anagram they'll know who played the trick on the Master of Peterhouse.'

'Trick? But I haven't been near Peterhouse. Oh, my God!'

For the first time, Sophie looked surprised. Still fuming, but now surprised. I picked up the phone and dialled Batty's number.

'Check our Scrabble set!' I whispered to Sophie.

'Hello? Ah, Lizzie. Will you do something for me? This is David, here. Sophie sends her love. Now go to your Scrabble set and get out all the letters for me, and count them with me will you? Yes, yes, I'm absolutely fine, Lizzie. Just got back from the Glasgow Seminar, so I'm a bit trussed up, but what with one thing and another I won't hold you up. I'll just hang on till you fetch your Scrabble set.'

'Here it is,' said Sophie, and poured out the letters from the little blue bag on to the table.

'Hello, Lizzie? I want you to count out your letters. Put them all in order, I'm waiting. A – should have nine. You can only find seven. Now D, don't worry about the Bs and Cs. You can only find one. You're sure? Yes, I know there should be four. Have you seen today's local paper? According to today's paper, my dear Lizzie you should have four, but you only have one. We should have four, and we have four. Yes, I'm fine. Just have a word with Sophie to confirm those figures, will you? She thinks I'm round the twist. Oh, and Lizzie, when Batty comes home tonight, ask him why there's only one D in his Scrabble, won't you? I'd really love to hear what he says.'

I handed the phone over to Sophie in some amusement, but she silently replaced the instrument on its cradle.

'D DID GIVE B A HIDING,' I misquoted. 'Your best friend's husband is the most notorious hoaxer since Horace de Vere Cole, and you automatically blame me! Can't you understand he was trying to fool the public as well as the Master? I'd better phone the Master's Lodge, and put them straight.'

'I thought there was a code of honour among schoolboys,' said Sophie, maliciously.

'There was – among schoolboys. But Batty's out of short trousers now, you know, and I'll be out of a job if it gets around that someone has worked out the anagram. Someone else.'

I skimmed through the phone book. Ah, Thomas, Sir John Meurig, Master's Ldg, Peterhouse, 39066.

'Sir John? Ah, well in that case could you kindly give him a message as soon as possible. I think he'll be very interested. My name is McMan, and I'd like to confess to putting a milk-float in his dining-room last night. The anagram was an attempt to incriminate an excellent scholar, young David Quitregard of King's. Ah. I'll spell that, of course. K,i,n,g, apostrophe s. Ah. Q,u,i,t,r,e,g,a,r,d. The culprit, that is to say my own name is Batty, spelt B,a,r,t,h,o,l,o,m,e,w. McMan spelt M with or without the a, c, capital M again, a, n. Have I lost you? Capital M,a,c, capital M,a,n. No, I can't suggest what to do with the milk-float unless you care of course to have it delivered back to me at my office in Cambridge Science Park.'

I carefully spelt out the address of his father's firm, where Batty worked. 'See he gets it in the morning, will you?'

Sophie would have smiled, but she has acquired a virtuous face from copying the portraits in Foxe's *Book of Martyrs*, and changed the subject.

She rehearsed, in alternating tears and angry reproaches, the calumnies that had been heaped anonymously on my head by someone – obviously other than Batty, engaged elsewhere – who had decided that if she or he couldn't have me, then I couldn't have Sophie. Was it the anonymous woman in the taxi from the Burrell, Neil Strutt, Tamara Ransome, Julia Baneath? Was Rose Calder, now Napcott, tired of my phone calls to Newport Post Office? Could I have been denounced by Miriam Blumenfeld, Mrs Tax, by Margot Liddell or her social worker?

Sophie said, 'I've been to see Salt and McPhee about a divorce. They say that in the case of irretrievable breakdown, I can petition for divorce on the grounds of two years' separation plus your consent, five years' separation without your consent, two years' desertion, unreasonable behaviour, or adultery.'

'Are you claiming unreasonable behaviour?'

She ignored this. 'I'm to claim maintenance for myself and the children, send my marriage certificate and the court fee. If you want to fight the divorce petition, it goes to the High Court, we both lose a lot of money, and I'd win anyway. If you don't fight it, the county court registrar puts the case before a local judge. After the decree nisi it takes six weeks for the decree absolute to end the marriage so I can start again.'

'Don't you think we should see a marriage guidance counsellor first?'

'What for? To ask whether playing around with other women is grounds for divorce? To ask them to patch things up, so you can carry on the same as before?'

'Do you want to sell the house?'

'Yes, if you don't want to give it to me. If you don't contest the proceedings, I'll give you half of the money from the sale.'

'We'll both lose.'

'This may be repeating the obvious – but you should have thought of that before.'

The phone rang. I answered it. It was Sophie's mother. They chatted about common friends and enemies, the weather, and above all Neil's feeding habits, an unquenchable source of curiosity to both of them.

When the tales of Pampers and pampered had clicked to a close, I returned to the attack.

'If I've been accused of something, like the milk-float in Peterhouse, I've got to be confronted with the evidence. Listen to the defence, as well as to the prosecution. Innocent until found guilty, and so on. Tell me what *you* were doing while I was in Glasgow.'

'I know you've been under strain since your parents passed away.'

'Died.'

'And I know men are supposed to be unfaithful.'

'But it's not compulsory.'

'How can you go out with another woman?'

'Easy. If you divorce me, I'm off to the Singles Club at Ely.'

'If not?'

'I'll stay at home with you and look after the family. Is there any mail from … the Faculty?' I couldn't say from Corinne, because she would only have got the wrong idea. You know what women are like.

And the funniest thing of all was, when I happened to go into Newport Post Office a year or so later, I found a faded, dogeared old card up on the notice-board that had clearly been there for months.

TITHE BARN ANTIQUES, it read. 9.30–5; Sundays 2–5.

And when I strolled up the High Street, the sign had been taken down and the place was a tea-shop.

'Yes,' said Mr Flack, back in the Post Office. The card had been paid for twelve months in advance. Forwarding address?

I don't know. You might try Mrs Napcott's brother. He's called Martin Calder. Works at Papworth Hospital. Believe he spends a lot of his time at Welney Marshes.'

I backed out of Newport Post Office. For the last time.

36

'Blanche Afanasian, Sufism and Modern Egyptian Literature …'

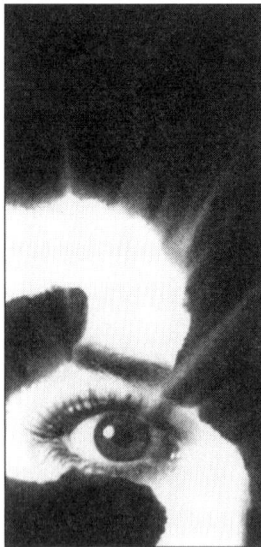